THE SHOOTING SCRIPT

PIECES OF APRIL

THE SHOOTING SCRIPT®

PIECES OF APRIL

SCREENPLAY AND NOTES BY
PETER HEDGES

A Newmarket Shooting Script® Series Book

NEWMARKET PRESS • NEW YORK

FIRST EDITION

03 04 05 10 9 8 7 6 5 4 3 2 1

ISBN: 1-55704-604-2 (paperback)

Library of Congress Catalog-in-Publication Data is available upon request.

QUANTITY PURCHASES

Companies, professional groups, clubs, and other organizations may qualify for special terms when ordering quantities
of this title. For information, write to Special Sales, Newmarket Press, 18 East 48th Street, New York, NY 10017;
call (212) 832-3575 or 1-800-669-3903; FAX (212) 832-3629; or e-mail mailbox@newmarketpress.com.

Website: www.newmarketpress.com

Manufactured in the United States of America.

CONTENTS

In memory of my mother,
Carole Hedges

INTRODUCTION

BY PETER HEDGES

In my basement, there are boxes and boxes of half-finished original screenplays. Notes, outlines, research. Rough drafts of the hand-model movie, the lip-sync movie, the movie about making a movie. Over the years, I became convinced I'd never be able to write an original screenplay.

I'd written probably too many plays, two novels, and several screenplay adaptations. What was the problem? I didn't understand until recently. I hadn't found the story I *had* to tell.

Here's how I found it.

In the late 1980s I lived in an apartment with an undependable oven. It seems there was an epidemic of undependable ovens because it was around that time I heard about a group of young people who were celebrating their first Thanksgiving in New York City. They went to cook the meal but the oven didn't work, so they knocked on doors until they found someone with an oven they could use.

I remember thinking this could be an interesting way to have all sorts of people cross paths who normally wouldn't. Because the beginnings of an idea can be fragile, I should've waited before I shared this broken oven premise with a friend. "It's a sketch," she said. I must have believed her because I promptly forgot about it. Or so I thought.

In December of 1998, I received a phone call from my mother in Iowa. She had bad news. She'd been diagnosed with cancer. I went to her as soon as I could. She underwent radiation and chemotherapy. Over the next fifteen months, my sister, my brothers, and I traveled back and forth to take care of her.

During this time, my mother urged me to keep writing, but it was difficult. One day in my office in Brooklyn, I started opening files on my computer and came across notes I'd written a year earlier for a story about a girl with a broken oven trying to get her turkey cooked.

In my notes, I had named the girl April after the moody, unpredictable month. The month when it is sunny one moment and rainy the next. In my notes, she was cooking Thanksgiving dinner for her family. Most surprising was the reason why I'd decided April was making the meal: She was attempting to bridge an estranged relationship with her mother who was sick with cancer.

That's when I knew this was a story I had to write.

★ ★ ★

If you're reading this introduction right now, perhaps you're a person who writes screenplays or who wants to write screenplays or maybe you love movies and are curious about how *Pieces of April* came to pass.

Hopefully, some of what you'll read will serve as a model of possibility. The goal is to be useful, which is why I've chosen to publish the shooting script as opposed to a transcription of the finished film. This way you can see how factors such as time, conditions, and other people's good ideas helped improve what was originally written. Following the Shooting Script, you'll find Scene Notes that detail the reasons for these changes.

★ ★ ★

Getting *Pieces of April* made was its own particular adventure, and I'll try to keep it brief.

On three different occasions, we were about to start production with a budget anywhere from $4-7 million. Each time it fell apart. In our third incarnation, we were even setting up production offices in Toronto, hiring designers and crew. I returned to Brooklyn for a few days to pack for the eight weeks of prep and the five-week shoot. That's when the call came. The number crunchers at the studio were shutting us down. We were back at the beginning, but for me it felt like the end. Fortunately, John Lyons, my stellar producer, suggested we call Gary Winick and Alexis Alexanian at InDigEnt, a company that makes digital films on a shoestring budget. They spoke with their partners, Caroline Kaplan and Jonathan Sehring at IFC Productions, and the irrepressible John Sloss, and in less than twenty-four hours, we were, as they say, "greenlit."

We met with them early the following week and they explained the limitations of budget and time. An abbreviated prep, sixteen shooting days, a ten-week post. This would be bare-bones filmmaking. We didn't hesitate. It was now or never. We signed on and we felt excited. John Lyons and I both started our creative lives by working in the theater. John worked for many years as a casting director at Playwrights Horizons and Manhattan Theater Club. Early in my writing career, I had a theater company called the Edge Theater. Along with Mary-Louise Parker, Joe Mantello, and others, we performed my plays in any theater we could rent for cheap. In truth, my happiest times were those poor days where we made work out of seemingly nothing. I felt that making *Pieces of April* with these limitations would be like a visit home. And it was.

When you can't offer huge salaries and the comfort of trailers and other perks, you find out who really wants to make the movie.

Katie Holmes had been a part of *Pieces of April* from the beginning. If anyone was justified in moving on, it was Katie. It's a testament to her that she stayed with us. Patricia Clarkson has been one of my favorite actresses for years. She was set to play Joy up in Toronto and when our circumstance changed, she didn't waiver. All of the other actors came on board with a clear idea of our situation. Oliver Platt loved the role of Jim and wanted the experience of shooting on digital video. Sean Hayes called from California, so eager to play Wayne that he offered to pay his way to New York to audition. "No need," I told him. "You've just been cast." At the last minute, we used John Lyons' frequent flyer miles to fly in a then-unknown Derek Luke to read for Bobby. His audition was transcendent. And so it went.

I'm often asked how much *Pieces of April* cost to make. A simple answer is difficult because it doesn't fully represent the truth. In dollars, maybe not so much. But, you see, for every person who worked on

Pieces of April, there's a story of sacrifice. So I don't know how to answer the question other than to say, "It cost a great deal."

★ ★ ★

If I gave a proper thank you to the many people who have impacted my writing life and this script in particular, this introduction would be longer than the script. So I'm going to dispense with the lengthy list of those to thank. However, no movie is made alone. And in my life as a writer, everything I've written has been improved by a cadre of good, smart friends. For years I've been helped by three incredible assistants — Sydney Sidner, Raymond T. Shelton and, most recently, Kirsten Schatz. Each of them impacted *Pieces of April,* and me, in unimaginable ways. Thanks also must go to Marc H. Glick for nineteen years of being my lawyer and friend; to Lucy Barzun, for her tenacity in all things good; and especially to Dianne Dreyer for keeping her promise. Years ago when she was the script supervisor on *What's Eating Gilbert Grape*, she swore that when I directed my first movie, she would be at my side. And she was.

Mostly I'd like to thank my wife, Susan Bruce, and our boys, Simon and Lucas, who sacrificed more than anyone to let me make this movie. If any of it works, it's because of them.

Finally, just so we're clear: This isn't an autobiographical story. I'm not April, and the character of April's mother is almost antithetical to my mother, who was warm and gentle. But all stories are seasoned by life, and this one is no exception. The one thing you do feel when someone you love is dying is the loud tick of time.

I wanted to make a movie about how we're running out time, and how we say—without words—thank you, and I'm sorry, and goodbye.

Pieces of April

by

Peter Hedges

March 25, 2002
Shooting Draft

1   INT. TENEMENT APARTMENT - ALPHABET CITY - NIGHT   1

A mixture of moonlight and streetlight streams through white,
lace curtains onto ...

APRIL BURNS, asleep and dreaming. She's a 21-year-old girl,   *
with dyed hair which she wears in a wild style, heavy   *
eyeliner, a pierced navel, and a tattoo of a lightning bolt
on her neck.

Next to her, a YOUNG BLACK MAN (also asleep) rolls over and
his arm falls gently across April's neck. This is BOBBY,
April's boyfriend. He wears short dreadlocks.

Close on April, still asleep. Her breathing accelerates.

2   APRIL'S DREAM   2

Blurry, at first. Something is moving. Something with brown   *
feathers, a red beak, beady eyes. Not one, but many turkeys   *
move about in a pen.   *

April stands in the middle of the turkey pen. (Or not.) She   *
looks at the camera. She gestures for us to come closer. We   *
do. She gestures for us to follow.   *

When she comes to a large tree stump (or bench), she sits,   *
lies back, brushes her hair to the side, looks up at us.   *

With one hand, April lightly, seductively touches her neck.   *

Camera Whips around to catch a glare from the blade of an axe   *
being raised.   *

April smiles, as if nothing would make her happier.   *

The Axe begins to move toward April's exposed neck ...   *

The screen goes momentarily white. We hear the sound of THE   *
AXE HITTING WOOD. And the FRANTIC FLAP OF TURKEY WINGS.   *

                                        END DREAM/RETURN TO:

April taking in a quick, desperate breath as her eyes *snap*   *
open.

                              SCREEN TO BLACK/TITLE CREDIT: *

3   OMITTED   3   *

4   INT. APRIL'S APARTMENT - LATER THAT MORNING   4   *

April has pulled the bed sheets tight up over her head.   *

Bobby sits on the edge of the bed.

                    BOBBY   *
            Hey. You. Come on. We need to get   *
            going.

April shakes her head. Beat. Bobby considers.   *

                    BOBBY
                (scooping her up)
            OK, then ...

5   INT. APRIL'S APT. - KITCHEN/LIVING ROOM - MOMENTS LATER   5

Bobby carries April who is still wrapped in the sheet, across
the room.

April kicks and screams, "No, No!" as they move out of frame   *
and we hear the sound of the shower faucet being turned on.
April screams.

6   INT. APRIL'S APT. - KITCHEN/LIVING ROOM - MOMENTS LATER   6

Close on April, her hair wet, in a foul mood, smoking her   *
morning cigarette.   *

Behind her, Bobby rushes about preparing the kitchen for   *
cooking: takes out every pot and pan, food supplies.

                    APRIL
            OK, I'll be right there.   *
                (long beat, as she smokes)   *
            I'm coming.   *
                (beat as she stubs out her   *
                 cigarette, takes out another   *
                 and lights it)   *
            Here I come.   *

Beat as April doesn't move.

                            MUSIC. ROLL CREDITS.

7   <u>MONTAGE</u>   7

Close on the turkey as April's hands rip the plastic wrapping
off.

She washes the turkey in the sink.

She studies the instructions on the back of a box of stuffing   *
mix, moving her finger as she reads.   *

She tentatively slides a hand inside and begins to pull out
the guts.

The turkey guts are plopped into an old pan.

Meanwhile, Bobby sets a smaller pan, filled with water, on a
burner, turns on the gas, but there is no flame.

Striking a match, he lights the burner and the blue flame
shoots up.

April separates the heart, gizzard and pulls the meat from
the neck, drops them in the now boiling small pan of water.

In the middle of a great deal of mess, Bobby holds the turkey
as April tries to stuff it, using a long stalk of celery, big
chunks of onion, and a mix they made from a box.

She struggles to push metal 'needles' through the pink flesh
of the turkey legs.

As she's trying to use string to truss the legs, she and
Bobby begin to laugh. The turkey looks somewhat sad.

                    APRIL
          It doesn't fucking matter anyway.   *

                    BOBBY   *
          Yeah, it does --   *

                    APRIL   *
          Bobby, they're probably not even gonna   *
          come.

8   OMITTED   8   *

                                                                   *

9   INT. THE BURNS HOUSE - MASTER BEDROOM - ALTOONA, PA   9

Close on digital alarm clock as the numbers turn from 7:01 to   *
7:02. The alarm is BLARING.   *

A man's hand fumbles around attempting to turn off the alarm.
No luck. The hand hits the alarm twice, *hard*! Still, the
alarm BLARES.

Desperate, the hand finds the electrical cord, yanks it, and
the alarm suddenly stops.

JIM BURNS, a middle-aged man, holds the cord to the alarm
clock.

He reaches across the bed for ...

> JIM
> (half asleep)
> Joy?

He looks over the side of the bed. No Joy.

Camera follows Jim as he climbs out of bed, moves to the
bathroom. He passes a Styrofoam wig holder which stands wig-
less on the dresser.

> JIM
> (checking the bathroom)
> Honey?

10   INT. THE BURNS HOUSE - HALLWAY - MOMENTS LATER   10

Jim pulls on his clothes as he hurries down the hall, past a
wall of family pictures. Camera stops on a picture of April,
age 13. Sweet smile, pink sweater, clean, well-combed hair -
looking nothing like the April of now.

> JIM (O.S.)
> Where are you?

11   INT. HALLWAY - OUTSIDE BETH'S ROOM   11

Close on bedroom door with a light blue sign with bright pink
lettering: BETH'S ROOM.

Jim pushes open the door.

(CONTINUED)

11   CONTINUED: 11

                         JIM
              Beth, have you seen --

Jim's POV: BETH - April's younger sister - turns, half-   *
dressed, covers her exposed parts, shrieks...

                         BETH
              Dad!

Jim quickly pulls the door almost closed and speaks through
the crack.

                         JIM
              I can't find her.

12   INT. BASEMENT STAIRS   12

      The light turns on and Jim hurries down the steps.

13   INT. BASEMENT   13

      Jim moves through the impeccably organized laundry room and
      tool room.

      Close on a miniature Pennsylvania license plate with TIMMY
      stamped in embossed letters.

      Jim pushes open the door to Timmy's room.

      TIMMY, age 17, hair too long, half-dressed in his only suit,
      looks up suddenly. The camera that he's loading with film
      accidently goes FLASH.

                         JIM
              Where is she?

                         TIMMY
                    (a reflex)
              I don't know.
                    (then:)
              Who?

      Jim moves out into the middle of the basement.

                         JIM
                    (worried and annoyed)
              Joy!

14   INT. COAT ROOM - SAME   14

        Beth, now worried, opens the coat room.

                          BETH
                Mother?

15   INT. BASEMENT LAUNDRY ROOM   15

        Timmy, always worried, checks the laundry room.

                          TIMMY
                Mommy?

16   INT. GARAGE - SAME   16

        Jim opens the door from the house and looks into the   *
        immaculate garage. Off screen, we hear Beth and Timmy   *
        calling for their mother.   *

        Jim stops, sees something.

        Jim's POV: JOY BURNS, 42, sitting in the passenger seat of *
        the family station wagon, all dressed, waiting and ready to *
        go.   *

        Joy taps her wrist where a watch would be if she wore a   *
        watch.   *

        Jim, relieved, smiles.   *

                          JIM   *
                    (calling back)   *
                OK, everybody, let's move it!   *

17   OMITTED   17   *

                                                                  *

18   INT. APRIL'S APARTMENT - KITCHEN AREA   18

        A heavy box is set on the table. Bobby opens it.   *

        April looks troubled.   *

                                                        (CONTINUED)

                    BOBBY   *
I picked up a few things. Just some
essentials.

                    APRIL
You better not have decorations in there.

                    BOBBY
No -- they're in here.   *

He lifts up a huge plastic shopping bag.

                    APRIL
No, Bobby. *No.*   *

                    BOBBY   *
            (unpacking the box)
Dishes. They don't even match.
Silverware, nothing fancy.   *

He sets two small hand-painted ceramic turkeys on the table
in front of April. April freezes.   *

                  BOBBY (cont'd)
These are for Salt and Pepper. Aren't   *
they great?   *
            (beat)   *
What is it?   *

                    APRIL   *
My mom had those same ones when I was a   *
kid.

                    BOBBY
Yeah?   *

                    APRIL
The one time she let me hold them, she
said, "Be careful, they're worth more
than you are."

                    BOBBY   *
That's terrible.   *

                    APRIL   *
            (beat as she picks them up)
The next year they were gone.

                    BOBBY
What happened?

                    APRIL
A hammer I was holding fell on them.

Bobby smiles.   *

                    APRIL (cont'd)   *
            How much were they?

                    BOBBY   *
            They weren't cheap.   *

                    APRIL   *
            How much? *How much did they cost?*

                    BOBBY
            Fifty cents.

Ouch.

                    APRIL
                (smiling to cover)
            You got yourself a deal.   *

April turns and carefully places the turkey salt and pepper
shakers in the trash. She walks out of the kitchen.   *

18A   INT. APRIL'S APARTMENT - BEDROOM - MOMENTS LATER   18A   *

Bobby sits down next to the lump in the bed that is April.   *

                    BOBBY   *
            I'm sorry. I didn't know ...   *

He touches where April should be under the covers but she's   *
not there. From behind, April pounces on him.   *

                    BOBBY   (cont'd)   *
            Whoa, wait -- we got a lot to do.   *

                    APRIL   *
            At 375 degrees and fully stuffed, a   *
            fifteen pound turkey will take five hours   *
            to cook, if you figure 20 minutes a   *
            pound.   *

She pins him to the bed and kisses him.   *

                    APRIL (cont'd)   *
            Leave an hour to cool.   *

She kisses him again.   *

                    BOBBY   *
            So you're saying ...   *

                                                    (CONTINUED)

18A   CONTINUED: 18A

                            APRIL   *
                  We got time.   *

                                                             *

19   INT. THE BURNS HOUSE - GARAGE   19   *

      Close on Joy. She has big, warm, wet eyes. She's incredibly
      thin. She wears a wig and her best dress.

      Camera stays on her during the following:

      Off screen, Timmy comes into the garage first. We hear the   *
      car door open.

                            TIMMY (O.S.)
                  Hey, Mom, how you feeling?

                            JOY
                  Good.

                            TIMMY (O.S.)
                  That's good.

      Timmy holds open a bag full of rolls of unexposed camera
      film.

                            TIMMY (cont'd)
                  How'd I do?

                            JOY
                  You did good.

                            TIMMY
                  I thought you'd think so.

                            JOY
                  You got your camera?

                            TIMMY
                  Absolutely.

                            JOY
                  You sure?

                            TIMMY
                  Positively.   *

20   INT. THE BURNS HOUSE - BETH'S ROOM   20

Jim is struggling to zip up the back of Beth's dress, which
is too small.

                         BETH
                (overly sweet, always smiling)
           I'm just wondering if it isn't completely
           selfish of her. Asking us to come all the
           way to New York. I mean, should Mom even
           be traveling?

                         JIM
                (grunting as he tugs at the
                zipper)
           If not now, when.

                         BETH
           I don't disagree. It's just *I* offered to
           make the meal. But that would have been,
           I suppose, too easy. And honestly,
           Daddy, what makes her think she can cook
           all of a sudden? I don't remember her
           ever being in the kitchen. Besides, I'm
           the one the who got an A in Home Ec. And
           what about Grandma Dottie ...?

21   OMITTED   21   *

                                                                *

22   INT. APRIL'S APARTMENT - BEDROOM - MOMENTS LATER   22

April, mostly clothed, on top of Bobby. They fuck throughout
the following:

                         APRIL   *
           Mashed potatoes, gravy; sweet potatoes
           cut up, melt some butter, sprinkle on
           brown sugar; green bean casserole made
           with green beans, *duh*. This other dish
           made with layers of crushed crackers and
           oysters, *sounds hard, isn't*, you just dot
           it with butter and right before baking,
           barely cover it with hot milk; cranberry
           sauce, open the can, then *plop* in a
           serving dish, *how simple is that?*;
           Waldorf Salad, made with apples, celery,
           nuts, grapes and in a dressing mixed with
           mayonnaise and thinned with milk or cream
           and some sweetener.
                         (MORE)
                                              (CONTINUED)

22 CONTINUED: 22

                   APRIL (cont'd)
        A Relish tray - celery! Carrots!
        Various kinds of! Pickles! And.
        Olives!

April collapses on top of Bobby. Both of them are out of
breath.

                   APRIL (cont'd)   *
        And for dessert, Pumpkin pie, store
        bought, but from a very ... good ...
        store.

Bobby looks at her. He cracks up laughing, and she joins him.   *

23 INT. THE BURNS HOUSE - GARAGE 23 *

Joy still waits as Timmy is in the middle of emptying out the
entire contents of his back pack, including, most notably, a
large photo album, a mini-portable CD player with headphones,
and numerous CDs.

                   TIMMY   *
        I know it's right here, somewhere -

                   JOY   *
        What's taking them so long?   *

                   TIMMY   *
        Oh, it's here, you'll see.   *

                   JOY
        Honk the horn.

                   TIMMY
        I'm sure they'll be right out.

                   JOY
        Honk the horn, please.

                   TIMMY
        We'll wake the neighbors. And we -

                   JOY
        Fuck the neighbors! Honk the goddamn
        horn!

24 INT. THE BURNS HOUSE - BETH'S ROOM 24

Jim is still struggling with the zipper on Beth's dress.   *

                                  (CONTINUED)

24   CONTINUED:

                   BETH
You know, it's not your responsibility to
patch things up. It's up to *them* --

                   JIM
          (grunting as he tugs at the
          zipper)
Maybe this isn't a good idea.

                   BETH
Finally, you said it--

                   JIM
The dress, I mean.

                   BETH
Look, the dress isn't the problem. It'll
fit, OK? *It will fit.* It's April that's
the probl--

Jim gives a forceful tug, the zipper finally un-sticks,   *
catching some of Beth's skin. She *shrieks* in pain.

25   INT. THE BURNS HOUSE - GARAGE   25   *

The car horn BLARES as Joy is leaning over the front seat and
has both hands pressing on the steering wheel.

                   TIMMY
Mom, please ...!
          (seeing them)
OK, OK! Here they come.

Joy lets up on the car horn. She sits back.

We hear first the LOUD CLACK of Beth's heels on the concrete, *
getting louder as she approaches. Beth appears in frame,
her usual peppy self.   *

                   BETH
Hey, how you feeling?

                   JOY
Good.

                   BETH
Nauseous, dizzy?

                   JOY
I feel good.

                              BETH
                    How'd you sleep? Did you sleep?

                              JOY
                    I slept good.

                              TIMMY
                         (astonished, as if this never
                          happens)
                    The camera - it's not here.

                              JOY
                         (smiles, because it always
                          does)
                    Better hurry.

Timmy climbs out of the car and hurries back into the house.   *

                              BETH
                         (secretly)
                    Now you know, Mom, all you have to say
                    is, 'I don't feel up to it' and we'll all
                    understand.

26   INT. BURNS HOUSE - COAT ROOM - CONTINUOUS   26   *

Jim is about to turn off the last of the lights when Timmy   *
barges into the coat room off the garage.   *
                                                                    *
                              JIM
                    Now what?

                              TIMMY
                    Forgot my camera ...

                              JIM
                    Jesus, Timmy.
                         (as they slide past each other)   *
                    And where's your tie?

                              TIMMY
                    Do I have to wear a tie?

                              JIM
                    You're not asking me that. You did not
                    ask me that.

                              TIMMY
                    No, sir.

                                                        (CONTINUED)

26   CONTINUED:

                         JIM
                    (pulls Timmy close, with sudden
                     emotion)
               You realize, this is very likely the last
               time --

                         TIMMY
               Dad, please, your breath.

Timmy pushes past and goes inside. Jim turns and looks   *
toward ...

27   INT. BURNS HOUSE - GARAGE   27   *

Joy and Beth, waiting in the car.

                         BETH
               So no numbness or discomfort?

                         JOY
               No.

                         BETH
               Headaches?

                         JOY
               No.

                         BETH
               Nauseous? Dizzy?

                         JOY
               You asked that already.

                         BETH
               All you have to say is 'I don't feel up
               to it'...

                         JOY
               Oh, is that all I have to say.

                         BETH
               Do you feel sweaty, clammy? Are your
               hands cold? Warm? Are your fingers
               tingly? Because all you have to --

                         JOY
                    (forcing a smile)
               Beth, shut the fuck up.

We hear KNUCKLES TAPPING LOUDLY on the car window.   *

                                              (CONTINUED)

27 CONTINUED: 27

Joy turns to find Jim pressing his face extremely close to   *
the glass.   *

                         JIM   *
                  (grinning and shouting)
              Morning, honey - how you feeling?!

                                                                    *

27A EXT. THE BURNS HOUSE - GARAGE - MOMENTS LATER   27A   *

The garage door raises and the Burns family car backs out of   *
the driveway. The door is almost closed when Timmy emerges,   *
ducking just in time, with tie on and camera in hand. He   *
climbs in the car. The car backs out into the street and   *
drives off.   *

28 INT. APRIL'S APARTMENT - KITCHEN AREA   28

Bobby is outside of the bathroom where April is presently   *
occupied.   *

                        BOBBY   *
              And don't you think cloth napkins would   *
              be, uhm, better ...

                      APRIL (O.S.)   *
              Paper's fine.   *

                        BOBBY   *
              But I'm worried the paper kind will feel   *
              kind of papery ...

                      APRIL (O.S.)   *
              Do we have to talk about this now?   *

                        BOBBY
              I could pick up some cloth napkins while   *
              I'm out doing that thing I gotta do ...

                        APRIL   *
              You're going out?   *

                        BOBBY   *
              Yeah, there's this thing ...   *

The sound of the TOILET FLUSHING.   *
                                                                    *

(CONTINUED)

28   CONTINUED:

28

                    BOBBY (cont'd)   *
          But it's good, though. I think you'll   *
          like why --

                    APRIL
              (emerging from the bathroom,   *
               dressed for the day)   *
          No, I *want* you to go out. I want you to
          go out *now*.

                    BOBBY
          Sorry?

                    APRIL
              (hands Bobby his jacket)
          And I want you to stay out as long as
          possible. Don't come back till noon.   *

                    BOBBY
          But I want to help --   *

                    APRIL
          That's how you'll help me. Just go do
          your own thing. I'll be fine.   *

                    BOBBY
          But - but -

                    APRIL
          Bobby, Bobby -- it's gonna be easier   *
          without you.

29   EXT. GOLDEN ACRES RETIREMENT VILLAGE   29

Jim leads DOTTIE DOYLE, a woman in her early seventies, out   *
of the nursing home.

                    JIM
              (to Dottie, who walks oh so
               slowly)
          Watch your step. Take your time.

Beth stands near the car, waiting to greet Dottie.

From the back seat of the car, Timmy focuses his camera on
Beth and is about to take an unflattering picture of her when   *
she notices.

                    BETH
          Don't even think about it.

                                              (CONTINUED)

                JOY
            (to Beth)
He's doing it for me. For when I'm old,
so I can always remember this day.

Joy laughs at her joke, Timmy smiles, turns the camera toward
Joy and takes a picture.

              JIM (O.S.)
Watch your step, Dottie. Careful now.

              BETH
Hi, Grandma.

             DOTTIE
Hello, dear.

              BETH
I'm Beth, your granddaughter, Beth.

             DOTTIE
Nice to see you, sweetie.

Timmy quickly gets out of the car to help Dottie.

             TIMMY
Hi, I'm Timmy.

              BETH
Timmy is your grand*son*.

             DOTTIE
Well, you don't say.

Dottie gets situated in the seat directly behind Joy. Timmy
helps Dottie with her seat belt. As the belt CLICKS into
place, Dottie notices Joy.

           DOTTIE (cont'd)
I know you.

              JOY
Hi, Mom.
        (beat)
Did you eat?

30   INT. APRIL'S APARTMENT - KITCHEN AREA   30

April pulls down the stove door and begins to empty out the
various items presently stored inside: an assortment of pots
and pans, two sweaters, several pairs of shoes, and an old
plaster pink piggy bank.

Bobby stands in the doorway, holding his gas-powered,   *
motorized mini-scooter under one arm.   *

                    BOBBY
          See you later.   *

                    APRIL
          Don't do anything stupid.   *

Bobby pulls the door closed.   *

Then she crosses to the table where there's a chewed on   *
pencil and a piece of paper.   *

Close on the piece of paper. At the top it reads *What to do.*   *
Below the paper is completely blank. April writes *Preheat*   *
Oven.   *

April turns the knob for the oven to 375 degrees.   *

Then she returns to the paper and crosses out the words   *
Preheat Oven.   *

31   EXT. KRISPY KREME PARKING LOT   31

The neon green and red "Krispy Kreme" sign. Below it, in red
lights - HOT DONUTS NOW.

Everyone barks out their orders as Jim turns off the engine
and gets out of the car.

                    JOY
            (as if a young school girl)
          Hot, Jim. Get whatever's *hot*!

                    BETH
          I want the vanilla frosted ones with
          peanuts sprinkled on!

                    TIMMY
          A strawberry long john, please!

                    DOTTIE
          Shouldn't he be writing this all down?

                                                    (CONTINUED)

31   CONTINUED:

                    BETH
          Glazed, jelly-filled, creme-filled ...

                    JOY
          And do not forget the custard-filled with
          the chocolate on top!

                    JIM
          Just remember, everybody -- April's
          cooking.

                    JOY
               (beat)
          You better get an extra dozen glazed.

32   INT. APRIL'S APARTMENT - KITCHEN AREA   32

      April finishes writing "Mom" on the Thanksgiving-themed name
      card she has decorated. Beat as she looks at it. She tears
      it in two. Then writes "Joy" on the Thanksgiving-themed name
      card.

      She glances up at ...

      A small clock on her dining room table which reads 8:00.

      April crosses to the turkey pan sitting on the counter, lifts
      the pan and carries it to the oven. She opens the oven.

      She's about to slide the turkey in when she stops. Beat. She
      reaches in, feels for heat. Her hands touch the sides of the
      oven. Her hands touch the metal roasting rack.

      She checks the temperature knob. It's been turned to 375.

      She stares in confusion, then it hits.

                    APRIL
          Oh, no. No -   *

33   INT. APRIL'S APARTMENT - MOMENTS LATER   33   *

      April finishes dialing her phone. Under her breath, she   *
      mutters "Bobby, Bobby, Bobby" as she punches in the final   *
      numbers. Beat. She hears a faint ringing. Following the   *
      sound, she locates its source. It's coming from under   *
      Bobby's bag of decorations. *It's Bobby's cell phone.* April *
      may (or may not) throw the phone against the wall.   *

34   EXT. STREET IN ALPHABET CITY   34   *

We hear the ROAR of a motor as Bobby rides his gas-powered   *
mini-scooter down a graffiti-riddled, trash-covered Lower   *
East Side street. He turns onto Avenue D and disappears.   *

35   OMITTED   35   *

36   EXT. KRISPY KREME PARKING LOT   36

Everyone (even Jim) eats a donut. Beth takes big bites,
Dottie nibbles, Timmy eats only the frosting. But it's Joy
who especially savors her Krispy Kreme. She chews
luxuriously, her lips ringed with frosting.

Silence as they chew.

                    JOY
              (spoken slowly)
          So now tell me - how could anyone not
          believe in God?

37   EXT. INTERSTATE 280 - DELAWARE WATER GAP   37

Ground level POV: The Burns family car whizzes past, heading
toward New York.

                    JOSE'S PHONE MACHINE (O.S.)
          Hello, this is Jose, your super ...   *

38   INT. APRIL'S APARTMENT - KITCHEN AREA   38

April, on the phone, while at the same time she's on her   *
knees, her head in the oven, banging around trying to fix it.   *

                    JOSE'S PHONE MACHINE (O.S.)
          If you're calling with a problem, hang in
          there. I'll be back tomorrow. Happy
          Thanksgiving.

                                        DISSOLVE TO:

39   INT. ARRIL'S APARTMENT - KITCHEN AREA   39

April, on another call. The phone book is open nearby.

                                        (CONTINUED)

39   CONTINUED: 39

                         TAPED VOICE
              "We want you to know that your call is
              important to us. In an effort to serve
              you better, your estimated wait is ... *48
              minutes.*"

         Frustrated, April slams the phone down.   *

40   INT. GAS STATION BATH ROOM - DAY   40

         Joy is kneeling over the toilet bowl.

                         BETH (O.S.)
                  How you doing in there?   *

41   EXT. GAS STATION BATH ROOM - CONTINUOUS   41

         Beth, on the other side of the door.

         We hear the SOUND OF JOY THROWING UP.

                         BETH
                     (beat)
                  Good job.   *

42   INT. APARTMENT BUILDING - SECOND FLOOR HALLWAY   42

         April knocks on Apartment #12. No answer. She waits. She
         knocks again.

         April moves to Apartment #11 and starts to knock.

         In quick succession: She knocks on Apartment #8, #9 and soon
         she's smacking Apartment #10

         The Door to Apartment #9 opens behind her.

                         HALF ASLEEP MAN FROM APT. 9
                  If you keep knocking like that, you're
                  going to wake me up.

                         APRIL
                  That's the -- (idea)

                         HALF ASLEEP MAN FROM APT. 9
                  And you don't want to wake me up.

                                                        (CONTINUED)

42   CONTINUED: 42

The Man slams the door shut.

43   OMITTED   43   *
                                                                                   *

                                                                                   *

43A   EXT. GAS STATION - BURNS FAMILY CAR & PARKING LOT   43A   *

The family sit in the car waiting for Joy.   *

                          BETH   *
                     (hushed)   *
              If you want my opinion ...   *

                          TIMMY   *
              Nobody wants your opinion.   *

                          BETH   *
              I'm not talking to you, all right?   *
                     (to Jim)   *
              You should take charge and we should turn   *
              around ...   *

The passenger door opens and Joy climbs in.   *

                          JIM   *
              Hey, you -- We were a little worried ...   *

                          JOY   *
              Oh, sweetie, don't be. I'm great, I feel   *
              fine.   *

Joy gets in the car, puts on her belt.   *

                          JOY (cont'd)   *
              I'm the excited one now.   *

                          JIM   *
                     (beat, pleased)   *
              And why is that?   *

Joy opens her purse/bag.   *

                          JOY   *
              Well, let's see, we got Fritos, Cheetos,   *
              Double Stuffs.   *

                          JIM   *
              No, Joy --   *

(CONTINUED)

43A CONTINUED:

                   JOY
Twinkies. Ho Ho's.

                   JIM
        (as he snatches up the bags of
        junk food as fast as he can)
Stop. Enough. Stop it! This is not
right. Not when April's hard at work,
making all your favorites. Not when she
called to double check a particular
recipe. So let's just cut this out right
now.

Jim exits the car with the bags of junk food. Joy follows.

                  BETH
I bet she called collect. I will never
call collect.

                 TIMMY
Aren't you the most perfect thing ever?

                 DOTTIE
Did someone say 'April?'

                  BETH
Yes, Grandma. She's your other
granddaughter.

                 DOTTIE
I know. I thought she was dead.

                  BETH
No, we haven't killed her yet.

Angle on:

Jim crossing the parking lot to the nearest trash can. Joy
catches up as he finishes throwing away the bags of snacks.

                  JOY
But, honey, it's so wasteful.

                  JIM
OK, I'm only going to say this once.
        (beat)
We're going to have a very nice time.

                  JOY
You don't actually believe that.

                  JIM
It's possible, I think, yes.

(CONTINUED)

                    JOY   *
          Well, you're a better man than me.   *

                    JIM   *
          Better man, that's ...funny.   *

                    JOY   *
               (takes his arm as they start   *
                back for the car)   *
          Don't get me wrong, I'm glad we're going.   *

                    JIM   *
          Good.   *

                    JOY   *
          This way instead of April getting off the   *
          bus with some new piercing or some ugly   *
          awful new tattoo and, God forbid, stay   *
          overnight -- *This way* we get to show up,   *
          experience the disaster that is her life,   *
          smile through it, and before we know it,   *
          we're on our way back home.   *

                    JIM   *
          We don't know that it's a disaster.   *

                    JOY   *
          Oh, I know. Believe me, I know.   *

As Jim helps Joy back into the car.   *

                    JIM   *
          She's doing better.   *

                    JOY   *
               (to the riders in the back)   *
          Miss me.   *

                    TIMMY   *
          You bet.   *

                    JIM   *
               (getting in on his side)   *
          She's had a couple of real jobs. She's   *
          got a new place. And Eddie the Drug   *
          Dealer is history. In fact she's met a   *
          new guy ...   *

                    BETH   *
          Oh god.   *

                    JIM   *
          But he ... he sounds promising.   *

                                              (CONTINUED)

43A   CONTINUED: (3)

                    JOY   *
          And why is that?   *

                    JIM   *
          He just does.   *

                    JOY   *
          No, Jim, please - tell us why he sounds   *
          promising.   *

                    JIM   *
          Apparently this new guy -- Bobby --   *
          reminds her of ... me.   *

     Beat. Jim can't help but smile as he starts the car. As   *
     they drive off, Joy reaches into her bag.   *

                    JOY   *
          Ding Dongs, anyone? Snow balls. Lil'   *
          Debbies ...   *

                    JIM   *
          Joy!   *

44   INT. APRIL'S APARTMENT BUILDING - STAIRWELL - LATER   44

     One floor higher. Instead of knocking, April listens at each
     door, hoping to hear someone stirring.

     Outside of Apartment #19, April presses her ear to the door.
     She hears the SOUND OF SOMEONE TALKING. She knocks with
     urgency. She rings the door bell.

                    WOMAN   *
               (from behind door)
          Who is it?

                    APRIL
          I'm in #13 ...

     The door opens. Standing there is EVETTE, an imposing, forty-   *
     something black woman.   *

                    APRIL (cont'd)
          Hi. Uhm, yeah, I got a problem.

     Evette smiles.

                    MAN'S VOICE
               (From inside the apartment)
          Who is it?

                                              (CONTINUED)

44   CONTINUED: 44

                      EVETTE   *
          It's that new girl in #13, says she's got
          a problem.

                      MAN'S VOICE
          What?

                      EVETTE
          Problems, Eugene. The girl has problems.
          She white, she got her youth, her whole
          privileged life ahead of her. Oh, I am
          looking forward to hearing about her
          problems!

Evette laughs a deep, full laugh as April just stands there.

45   INT. EVETTE AND EUGENE'S APARTMENT (#19)   45

Close on April, finishing ...

                      APRIL
          So that's the short version ...

Angle on:

Evette as tears run down her face. Next to her sits EUGENE,
her husband. Moist in the eyes, he slips Evette a Kleenex.
Behind them, framed pictures of their many children and other   *
relatives hang on the walls.   *

                      EVETTE
          Oh my.

                      EUGENE
           God damn.

                      APRIL
           If I told you the long version, you
          wouldn't have cried.

                      EVETTE
           And she's how old?

                      APRIL
           She had me when she was my age, so she's   *
          forty-two.   *

                      EVETTE
           I'm forty-two.   *

45   CONTINUED: 45

                          EUGENE
             You're forty-five.   *

Evette shoots an annoyed look at Eugene.

                          EVETTE
             I can't imagine. Truth is none of us
             know. Eugene here could get to chewing   *
             on his supper and choke to death on a   *
             turkey bone this very day. We just don't
             know.
                  (beat)
             But to realize your time is almost up,
             and you have one last chance to do
             everything you love... and be with those
             you love...

                          EUGENE
             God damn.

Eugene stands up, goes to the kitchen area begins to bring
out the various foods and dishes to prepare their
Thanksgiving meal.

                          EVETTE
             You poor thing. Your poor mother.

                          APRIL
             Yes, no. Uhm.

                          EVETTE
             You two must have a special relationship.

                          APRIL
             Oh, we do. Yes! We're really close?
             More like sisters, really. I mean, she's
             my best --

                          EVETTE
             You don't get along, do you?

                          APRIL
             No.
             Not at all.
             Never have.

                          EVETTE
                  (beat)
             Oh, dear.

                          EUGENE (O.S.)
             Evette ...

                                              (CONTINUED)

45   CONTINUED: (2)   45

                         EVETTE
              I know, honey. I know.
                   (To April)
              Sweetie, we got our own meal to make.

                         APRIL
                   (getting up to go)
              Oh, OK. I underst--

                         EVETTE
              Don't you move.
                   (to Eugene)
              Tina's coming with the boys around two?

                         EUGENE
              That's right.

                         EVETTE
              And Glen will be late, as always. And do
              we even know if Rasheed's coming?

                         EUGENE
              I know what you're thinking.

                         EVETTE
              Of course you do, baby. You always know
              what I'm thinking.
                   (To April)
              Here's what. We'll hold off cooking ours
              till ten. That'll get you started. And
              it gives you two plus hours to find
              another oven. How's that sound?

     April fights smiling, then smiles.

46   INT. APRIL'S APARTMENT   46

     Close on paper as April finishes writing note. She writes:
     "Bobby, Stove broke! If not here, I'm in Apartment #19."

     She lifts the turkey, turns off the light, and, with her arms
     full, manages to close the door behind her.

47   EXT. STREETS OF THE LOWER EAST SIDE   47

     Bobby has stopped in front of a bodega, his motor still   *
     running. He looks about suspiciously, checks out the   *
     flowers for sale, and he's about to take off when he realizes *
     a BOY ON A BIKE is blocking his way.   *

                                              (CONTINUED)

47   CONTINUED: 47

Bobby turns off his motor.   *

                    BOY ON BIKE   *
          I got a message for you.   *

                    BOBBY   *
          Yeah?   *

                    BOY ON BIKE   *
          Tyrone's looking for you.   *

                    BOBBY   *
              (beat)   *
          I don't know Tyrone.   *

                    BOY ON BIKE   *
          Well, Tyrone knows you.   *

Beat. The boy laughs as he rides off on his bike.   *

Bobby watches, confused, then he starts his engine and takes   *
off uptown.   *

48   INT. EVETTE AND EUGENE'S APARTMENT   48

April hands the turkey pan to Evette, who carefully sets the   *
turkey down on the oven rack, slides it in, closes the oven
door. Meanwhile, Eugene continues prepping the kitchen.   *

                    EVETTE
          This is a nice thing you're doing for
          her.

                    APRIL   *
              (to herself)
          Not really.

                    EVETTE
          It is! It's a nice gesture. Isn't it
          nice, Eugene?

                    EUGENE
          I have a question.

                    APRIL   *
          'Nice' writes letters. 'Nice' goes home
          to visit.

                    EVETTE
          You haven't been back --

                                                          (CONTINUED)

                         APRIL
              Fuck no.

                         EUGENE
              I have a question.

                         EVETTE
              Not since she got (sick) --   *

                         APRIL
              She likes it that way.   *

                         EVETTE
              I don't believe you.

                         APRIL
              Believe me. I'm her first pancake.   *

                         EVETTE   *
              What do you mean?   *

                         EUGENE   *
              She's the one you're supposed to throw   *
              out.   *

Beat as Evette gets it.   *

                         EUGENE (cont'd)   *
              Now I have a question--   *

                         EVETTE
                   (impatient with Eugene)
              What?

                         EUGENE
              Did you stuff it?
                   (beat)
              Has the bird been stuffed?

                         APRIL
              Yes, *yes.*

                         EUGENE
              With what?

                         APRIL
              Stalk of celery, I don't know...

                         EVETTE
              Celery's good.

                         APRIL
              Chopped up chunks of onion...

                                              (CONTINUED)

                         EVETTE
              Onion's good.

                         APRIL
              Mostly it's a mix from the box.   *

                         EUGENE   *
                    (awkward beat)   *
              You used store bought stuffing?   *

                         APRIL   *
              Uhm, yeah. Is that bad?   *

Eugene grunts to himself.

                         EVETTE
              No, it'll be fine, *fine*.

                         APRIL
              What should I have --

                         EVETTE
              I'm sure it's a good brand. A *fine*
              brand.

                         EUGENE
                    (mumbles under his breath)
              You don't use store bought stuff-

                         EVETTE
              Oh, please, Eugene. Your first turkey.
              Need I remind you of that half cooked
              affair. The meat all pink, no flavor
              whatsoever. Then the next year, you
              burnt the poor bird --

49   INT. APRIL'S APARTMENT - KITCHEN AREA   49

April uses a manual can opener to open a can of cranberry
sauce.

She smacks the bottom of the can until it plops out, most of
making it into the bowl. The rest lands on the counter.

With her hands, she scoops the rest into the bowl.

She sets the cranberry sauce in the refrigerator.

She sets a large bag of potatoes on the counter, rips open   *
the plastic too far, and many potatoes tumble to the floor.

50   OMITTED   50   *
                                                                           *

50A   EXT. BURNS FAMILY CAR - INTERSTATE 280   50A   *

The Burns family car barrels down the highway. Jim drives,   *
Joy struggles unfolding a map. Dottie, Timmy and Beth are in   *
back.   *
                                                                           *

                    BETH   *
          Mom, what are you doing, Mom? Dad   *
          doesn't need a map.   *

                    JOY   *
          I want to go an alternate route. Back   *
          roads. See things we've never seen.   *
          That way this day will not be a complete   *
          waste.   *

                    JIM   *
          If that's what you want ...   *

                    JOY   *
          Besides we don't want to be early.   *

Joy finishes spreading the map out on her lap.   *

                    JOY (cont'd)   *
          Now I'm giving you a choice. I can   *
          either study the map or we can rely on my   *
          uncanny sense of direction.   *
               (beat)   *
          Now which will it be?   *

                                                                           *

51   OMITTED   51   *

                                                                           *

52   INT. APRIL'S APARTMENT - KITCHEN AREA   52

Close on April's hands using a small knife to peel a potato.
She cuts her finger.

Using a larger knife, she finishes chopping a potato into
small pieces. (Her finger is now bandaged.) She starts on a
second potato.

She uses her forearm to sweep a small mountain of peeled,
chopped potatoes into a bowl.

                                                        (CONTINUED)

52   CONTINUED: 52

She finishes writing *Prepare Potatoes* and then crosses it off   *
the "What to do" list.

53   INT. APARTMENT #19 -- EUGENE AND EVETTE'S KITCHEN   53

Evette has let April in to check on the turkey. Eugene is
busy preparing their food to cook.

                    EVETTE
          Careful. Don't let the heat out...   *

                    APRIL
          OK.

April opens and closes the oven door very fast.

                    EVETTE
               (smiling)
          How's it look?

April shrugs.

                    APRIL   *
          I wouldn't know.   *

April notices Eugene doing his food preparations. He is a   *
model of possibility. Organized and economical in his
movements, he's doing many tasks at once; chopping nuts,
washing vegetables, preparing his stuffing.

                    APRIL (cont'd)   *
          What's he making?

                    EVETTE
          Tell her what you're making, Eugene.

                    EUGENE
               (beat as he continues working)
          Nothing special this year.

                    EVETTE
          No...
               (unable to hide her pride)   *
          Just sweet potato soup with buttered
          pecans. Herbed oyster stuffing, giblet
          gravy. Diced carrots, turnips. Some
          lemon rosemary green beans. Sauteed red
          Swiss chard with garlic. Hickory Nut Ice
          Cream. Maple Pumpkin Pie.

                                                      (CONTINUED)

>   APRIL
>   (genuinely impressed)   *
>   Wow.

>   EVETTE
>   'Nothing special this year.'

>   APRIL
>   (laughing)
>   Yeah, right.

>   EVETTE
>   How about you?

>   APRIL
>   No. Well, uhm, turkey, gravy. Waldorf
>   Salad?

>   EVETTE
>   Ooo. Waldorf Salad. That sounds
>   *unusual.*

>   APRIL
>   It's made with different fruits, nuts.
>   The dressing's pretty much just
>   mayonnaise. And I'm making mashed   *
>   potatoes, of course. And cranberry
>   sauce, which was easy –
>   (a joke attempt)
>   You just open the can!

>   EUGENE
>   (stops working, not believing
>   what he's hearing)
>   Evette?

>   EVETTE
>   (to April)
>   Oh, sweetie...

>   APRIL
>   But I like it from the can.   *

>   EUGENE
>   Nobody likes it from the can.

April looks to Evette for help.

>   EVETTE
>   This time I'm going to have to agree with
>   Eugene.

54   INT. APRIL'S APARTMENT - KITCHEN AREA   54

April pulls open the refrigerator door. She removes the dish
of cranberry sauce, turns over the bowl, and the cranberry
sauce falls, *plop*, into the trash.

55   EXT. SHOULDER OF COUNTRY ROAD   55

The Burns car has stopped again. Jim rolls down the driver's
side window. He leans out to hear better.

                    TIMMY (O.S.)
            It was a squirrel, I think. Or a very
            small raccoon.

Joy taps Jim's shoulder. Jim turns to look at her.

                    JOY
            Honey?

                    JIM
            Yes, Joy.   *

                    JOY
            Hop to.

56   EXT. SIDE OF ROAD / BURNS CAR - MOMENTS LATER   56

The back door of the station wagon is raised. Jim pulls out
a garbage bag. Two pairs of rubber gloves. A small garden
shovel. Timmy arrives for the gloves.

                    TIMMY
            She found a good spot.   *

57   EXT. SIDE OF THE ROAD - MOMENTS LATER   57

Close on Jim as he finishes covering the dirt over the hole.
He pats it down with his foot.

Wide Shot:

We see that Joy and Beth have joined Jim and Timmy. Dottie
remains in the car.

                    JOY
            Timmy?

                                            (CONTINUED)

> TIMMY
>   (bowing his head in prayer)
> Uhm. Well. We're sorry we didn't know
> you. We hope it was quick. And ...

> JOY
> That's fine. Beth? A song?

> BETH
>   (annoyed)
> *No.*

Joy looks to Jim.

> JIM
> I think Timmy pretty much said it all.

> JOY
>   (beat)
> Then what are we waiting for?

                                        SMASH CUT TO:

58   EXT. COUNTRY ROAD   58

Burns car zips past, water from puddle ... SPLASH.

59   INT. APARTMENT #19 -- EUGENE AND EVETTE'S APARTMENT   59

Evette is teaching April how to make homemade cranberry
sauce. Unnoticed by the two women, Eugene's activities grow
more frantic as he tries to cook around them.

> EVETTE
> Pour it in, sweetie ...

April pours in a cup of sugar.

> EVETTE (cont'd)
> Look at you. You're a natural.

> APRIL
> Oh, right.

> EVETTE
> Now then while we wait for it to
> dissolve, you stir ...

Evette hands April a wooden spoon and she begins to stir.

                                              (CONTINUED)

                    EVETTE (cont'd)
          You go, girl!

                    APRIL
          Stop, I'm doing nothing.

                    EVETTE
          Have you done it before?

                    APRIL
          No.

                    EVETTE
          Then it's not nothing.

                    EUGENE
               (needing to reach past them)
          Excuse me ...

                    APRIL
          What's next?

                    EVETTE
          We're going to let it simmer until it's a
          lovely texture.

                    EUGENE
               (slightly agitated)
          Please, can you ...

                    APRIL
          And then ...

                    EVETTE
          Then we wait for it to cool off...

                    EUGENE
          Ladies, please!

                    EVETTE
          Honey, just use your words and tell us,
          we'll move.

          April and Evette step out of the way as Eugene needs access
          to the sink. Evette takes April by the arm and leads her
          into the living room.

                    EVETTE (cont'd)
               (quietly)
          Eugene always gets a little fussy.
          Have you had any luck finding another--

                                               (CONTINUED)

                         APRIL
          I haven't even started.

                         EVETTE
          Because probably the sooner you --

                         EUGENE (O.S.)
          Evette, where's --

                         EVETTE
          -- can find another oven --

                         EUGENE (O.S.)
          The rolling pin!

                         EVETTE
          The better.

                         APRIL
          Don't worry. Done.

60   INT. APRIL'S APARTMENT BUILDING - HALLWAY   60

OUTSIDE APARTMENT #17

The door is opened a crack, an OLD MAN peers out. A chain
lock keeps the door from opening further.

                         APRIL
          Eugene and Evette in #19 - do you know
          them? - they're helping me out for the
          time being, and I was wondering --

61   OUTSIDE APARTMENT #18   61   *

A COUPLE, trying to leave with bags for a weekend trip. By   *
the way they're half listening, and because the Man is about
to lock his door, it doesn't look particularly promising.

                         APRIL
          See, my family's coming -- my mom's very --
          it's complicated ...
               (laughing nervously)
          and then the *stove* ... or the *oven* ... I
          don't know what it's called ... the
          bottom part --

62   OUTSIDE APARTMENT #20   62

A large MAN IN A MOHAIR SWEATER stands in front of his
apartment. He listens as April finishes her plea.

                    APRIL
          The truth is she's a rotten mother so I
          don't know why you'd even want to help
          me.

                    MAN IN MOHAIR SWEATER
               (beat)
          You know, it's funny. My mother was a
          mean woman, too. Naaasty. There wasn't
          a nice bone in her body.

                    APRIL
          Oh?

                    MAN IN MOHAIR SWEATER
          She smoked non-stop, cheated at cards,
          and she complained every day of her life--

                    APRIL
          Gosh, I'm sorry.

                    MAN IN MOHAIR SWEATER
          And you know what?
               (suddenly emotional)
          There's nothing I wouldn't do for a
          chance to spend some more time with her.

                    APRIL
               (beat)
          So you'll help me?

                    MAN IN MOHAIR SWEATER
          Mi casa es su casa.

The Man holds open the door for April. Inside, and this
cannot be emphasized enough, it's an absolute pit.

April's POV: Stacks of newspapers, garbage overflowing from
the trash can, but most noticeable, *big balls of fur*. These
balls of fur are actual living cats. *Many* cats. Jumping
from the top of the refrigerator, cats on the counters, cats
kicking an empty cat food can across the floor.

April stares, stunned.

63   OUTSIDE APARTMENT #22   63

April knocks as she calls through an unopened door.

                    APRIL
               (faintly)
          I wonder if you could ... *help*.

64   EXT. STREETS OF HARLEM   64   *

Bobby at a pay phone, holding a scrap of paper with a phone
number.

                    BOBBY
          Latrell? Is Latrell there? Tell him
          Bobby called. Tell him I'm waiting where   *
          he said. What? Yeah, he knows what it's
          about.

Bobby hangs up the phone.

65   INT. APARTMENT HALLWAY   65

April follows after TISH, a colorfully dressed hippy type.

                    APRIL
          Oh, great. Really, it's a big help.
          You don't know what this means.

                    TISH
               (keeps walking)
          Good.

                    APRIL
          By the way, I'm April, in #13.

                    TISH
               (disappearing up the stairs)
          Tish in #24.

                    APRIL
          Thank you, Tish in #24.
               (to herself)
          Thank you, I thank you, my family thanks
          you ...

66   EXT. ROADSIDE ATTRACTION (TO BE DETERMINED)   66

Timmy focuses his camera which is mounted on a tripod.
He sets the automatic timer. He hurries out of the frame
toward ...

Reverse Angle on:

Joy, Beth, Dottie, and Jim who pose in front of / or next to
a large or not-so-large roadside attraction or possibly just
a beautiful tree.

                    JIM
              (once Timmy has joined them)
         Smile, everybody. We only have time for
         one.

POV through Timmy's camera lens:

We hear the LOUD TICK of the Automatic Timer.

While the Burns family (those present) waits for the click,
their smiles go from sincere to forced, from pleased to
pained. For them it becomes an excruciating wait.

Finally, there's the click.

Whew.

                    JOY
         That will be our Christmas card.

                    JIM
              (following after Joy towards
               the car)
         Without April?

                    JOY
         It's good to have options.

67   INT. APRIL'S APARTMENT - KITCHEN AREA   67

April dumps out Bobby's big plastic bag of decorations.
Streamers, Balloons, fold-out paper Pilgrims.

April finishes blowing up a balloon. She ties it.

There's a KNOCK ON THE DOOR. She flicks the balloon with her
finger and it floats and lands with several other blown-up
balloons.

                                              (CONTINUED)

April opens the door to find Evette standing in the doorway,
holding the *turkey pan*.

> EUGENE (O.S.)
> (calling from two flights up)
> Evette, where's the strainer!

Evette extends the turkey pan.

> EVETTE
> Good luck.

68   INT. APRIL'S APARTMENT   68

Close on April's message to Bobby. April crosses out the *#19*
and writes *#24*.

69   EXT. STREETS OF HARLEM   69   *

Bobby stands waiting by the pay phone. No sign of Latrell.
Growing restless, Bobby kicks a city trash can.

70   INT. DOOR OUTSIDE APARTMENT #24   70

April uses hot pad holders to carry the turkey pan. With her
hands full, she uses her forehead to knock on the door.

Tish opens the door.

> APRIL
> It's just me.

> TISH
> Oh. Can I talk to you for a second?

> APRIL
> Sure.

> TISH
> Alone.

April is perplexed.

Tish indicates the turkey.

> APRIL
> Yeah, OK.

(CONTINUED)

70   CONTINUED:

April reluctantly sets the turkey down outside and steps into
the doorway, maybe keeping the door ajar with her foot so she
can keep her eye on the turkey.

                    TISH
          There's something I need you to know.

                    APRIL
          OK ...

                    TISH
          I never eat anything that has a face.

                    APRIL
          Don't worry. You won't be eating it.
          I'll just be using your oven --

                    TISH
          Yes, but for me to know that there was
          once a living, breathing soul --

                    APRIL
          I'm a vegetarian, I understand --

                    TISH
          Yes, but I'm a vegan. And even the smell
          of flesh cooking makes me --
          I don't think I can help you.

Close on April standing there, not knowing what to say.

                    TISH (O.S.) (cont'd)
          Now I do have a great recipe for a
          Meatless Nut Roast.

71   EXT. A STREET ON THE LOWER EAST SIDE   71

Bobby, at the pay phone again.

                    BOBBY
                 (on phone)
          I'm just wondering if maybe Latrell
          forgot, that's all ... hello?   *

Bobby slams the phone into the receiver five times fast.   *

                                                               *

72   INT. APARTMENT HALLWAY - FOURTH FLOOR   72

April moves quickly to each door on the fourth floor,
knocking on Apartment #26, #27, #28.

                    APRIL
               (as she knocks)
          Can anybody hear me? Is anybody home!
          Please! Please somebody!

April stops, turns sees an OLD WOMAN sticking her head out of
Apartment 26. She's talking but she can't be heard. She
wears a macrame scarf around her neck which covers the fact
that she has no voice box.

                    APRIL
               (straining to hear)
          Talk louder, lady.

The Old Woman holds up a device to her throat which amplifies
her robot-like sounding voice.

                    AN OLD WOMAN
          Try Wayne in 30. He's got a new stove.

April turns away from the Woman and finds the door to
Apartment #28 open. A CHINESE MAN, in his mid-fifties, looks
out. TWO CHILDREN peer around the door as well.

                    APRIL
          Hi. Hello. Listen. I need. This.

April holds up the turkey.

                    APRIL (cont'd)
          If I could borrow your (stove) ...

                    MAN (O.S.)
          They don't speak English.

                    APRIL
               (without looking at the Man)
          I know that!
               (not missing a beat, speaks
                more slowly)
          If.
               (points to her chest)
          I. Could. Borr(ow)--

                    MAN (O.S.)
          You're wasting your time.

                                        (CONTINUED)

72   CONTINUED: 72

April turns to see a SLIGHTLY ODD, SOMEWHAT CREEPY-LOOKING
MAN, mid-thirties, dressed crisply, wearing a toupee. The   *
Man holds a small dog. The Man disappears up the stairs.   *

Camera follows April as she goes after him.

73   INT. APARTMENT BUILDING HALLWAY - TOP FLOOR   73

April appears as the Man is taking out his keys to unlock his
Apartment. It's Apartment #30.

                    APRIL
          Excuse me. Are you Wayne?

Man says nothing.

                    APRIL (cont'd)
          Wayne with the new stove?

The Man turns, smiles.

74   INT. APARTMENT #30 (WAYNE WITH THE NEW STOVE)   74

Close on the New Appliance. Bright white, gleaming, sunlight
bounces off the six stainless steel burners.

                    WAYNE
          Technically it's a self-cleaning,
          convection *oven*. It's got an Automatic   *
          Meat Thermometer, Audible Preheat Signal,
          the Dual Bake Element, Hot Surface
          Lights, Roasting Rack. And my favorite,
          the Frameless Glass Oven Door with Deluxe
          Big View Window.

                    APRIL
          Wow. It's beautiful.   *

                    WAYNE   *
          Yes, it is.   *

                    APRIL   *
          It's so new. And shiny. And I don't   *
          know how to ask this --   *

                    WAYNE   *
          Be my guest.

                                              (CONTINUED)

74   CONTINUED: 74

                              APRIL
                     Really?

                              WAYNE
                     I'd be delighted.

As Wayne pushes the appropriate buttons to begin preheating
the oven, the dog begins to growl.   *

                              WAYNE (cont'd)
                     Shhh, Bernadette.

Bernadette growls louder, snaps at the air.

Wayne looks up at April, smiles.

                              WAYNE (cont'd)
                     Don't worry. She doesn't bite.   *

                                                                  *

75   INT. APRIL'S APARTMENT   75   *

Close on April's message to Bobby. April crosses out the   *
#24 and writes #30.   *
                                                                 *

76   EXT. STREETS OF THE LOWER EAST SIDE   76

Bobby is still at his spot, waiting.

Latrell, a small, wiry young man in his early 20's, steps up
behind him.

                              LATRELL
                     Boo.

                              BOBBY
                     Aw, man, come on. Where you been?

They punch each other in a playful way.

                              LATRELL
                     Where *you* been?

                              BOBBY
                     You're gonna make me late.

                              LATRELL
                     Then let's go already.

Bobby follows Latrell down the street.

                                                        (CONTINUED)

                    BOBBY
               (beat)
          Hey, do we know a Tyrone?

                    LATRELL
          I know two, but they're both upstate.
          Why?

                    BOBBY
          It's nothing.
          Do we have far to --

                    LATRELL
               (stops, points)
          Nope, there she is.

                    BOBBY
               (stops, looks to where Latrell
                points)
          You got to be kidding, right? Tell me
          you're kidding.

A large sign in dark blue lettering reads: "GOODWILL"

Below the sign is a Goodwill Store.

77   EXT. GOODWILL - BACK DOOR - MOMENTS LATER   77

As Latrell unlocks the padlock, removes it and lifts the
security gate.

                    BOBBY
          You said you worked in retail--

                    LATRELL
          I didn't lie to you--

                    BOBBY
          You never said 'Goodwill'--

                    LATRELL
          I never said I didn't work at Goodwill--

                    BOBBY
          Quality men's clothes. You said you
          could get me a good deal on some *quality
          men's clothes*!

                    LATRELL
          If you're willing to look for it, there's
          a deal here.

                                              (CONTINUED)

77   CONTINUED: 77

                         BOBBY
              Aw, crap, Latrell.

                      LATRELL
         Man, I was wrong about you. I thought,
         here's a guy who doesn't need some
         designer label. Some Armani/Prada
         bullshit. There are hidden treasures
         here at the Goodwill. But only if you
         look for 'em, baby. Ninety per cent of
         the world would be happy with these
         clothes. The bad stuff? We don't hang
         onto the bad stuff. If it's useful, if
         it could be worn, if we could wear it or
         if someone we love could wear it, it goes
         on the rack! *Now if you're too good for
         Goodwill ...*
                   (beat as he goes in the store,
                    then turns)
         Well, then I can't help you.

Latrell enters the store.

                      BOBBY
                 (following after)
         Like I have a choice.

                      LATRELL
         Most of the time, my friend, we don't.
         So when we do, we best choose well. Now
         get looking. Were I you, I'd start over
         there.
                   (points to several racks of
                    Men's clothes)
         Were I you.

Bobby trudges over to the area where Latrell pointed. Now
inside, Latrell pulls the security gate down behind him.

78   EXT. COUNTRY ROAD   78

A bucolic, curved country road.

                      JOY (O.S.)
         Could you pull over? Jim. Pull over. Jim,
         now?

Beat. The Burns family car comes into frame and pulls off
onto the shoulder. Beth hops out and opens the passenger-
side door. She reclines Joy's seat. Joy lies back, closes
her eyes. She appears to be in some pain.

                                                 (CONTINUED)

                         BETH
                    (puts her hand to Joy's
                     forehead)
               You don't feel warm. Do you feel woozy?
                    (no answer)
               Did you take your meds?

Joy shakes the prescription bottle she's holding.

                         BETH (cont'd)
               Do you feel tired? Are you ...

                         JOY
               Beth -

                         BETH
               Sorry.

                         JOY
               It's just, I keep waiting for a good time
               to tell you. But there's really no good
               time.
                    (extremely serious)
               I need everyone to listen. Timmy.

Timmy takes off his headphones and turns off the portable CD
player. The mood in the car turns solemn, almost grim.

                         JOY (CONT'D) (cont'd)
               I don't know how to say this. We need to
               discuss how each of you ... oh god ...
               how each of you, in your own way, is
               going to handle ... discarding food
               without letting our hostess know.

Beat. Timmy smiles first. Beth is slow to get it. And Jim
doesn't like where this is headed.

                         JIM
                    (starting the engine)
               Joy, please --

                         JOY
                    (fights smiling)
               Here's my suggestion.

                         JIM
               Beth. The door.

                         JOY
               Take a bite of whatever it is. Let's
               say, the green bean casserole.
                    (MORE)

                                            (CONTINUED)

78   CONTINUED: (2)   78

                              JOY (cont'd)
                    Pretend to chew. Cough. Bring napkin to
                    mouth. Spit food into napkin. Excuse
                    yourself.

With Beth back in the car, Jim peals out onto the road.

                              JOY (O.S.) (cont'd)
                    Drop food into toilet. Flush.

We hear everyone but Jim laughing.

79   EXT. GAS STATION - DAY   79

Timmy is helping Joy, who is feeling nauseous, walk to the
Women's Room at the Gas Station.

Timmy holds open the bathroom door for Joy.

80   INT. GAS STATION BATHROOM - DAY - CONTINUOUS   80

As soon as they enter, Timmy pulls out a small bag filled
with marijuana and several already-rolled papers.

Silence as Joy waits. She doesn't feel well.

                              JOY
                    Honey, roll it tighter next time.

                              TIMMY
                    Sorry, Mom.

Timmy flicks his lighter, lights the joint.

Joy inhales.

81   EXT. GAS STATION - DAY   81

Outside of bathroom, Timmy turns toward the family car and
gives a thumbs-up.

START MUSIC: Smack Daddy's "Who the Foo are U!"

82   EXT. HIGHWAY   82

The Burns family car speeds onto the highway.

83   INT. THE BURNS FAMILY CAR   83

Close on Joy ...

Who wears the headphones from a portable CD, moving to the
beat of Smack Daddy's "WHO THE FOO ARE U." We hear what she
hears. She sings along.

Wide shot. We only faintly hear the music, but Joy's
shouting out fragments of the lyrics. "Baby sweet baby/I am
she/You're the one for me/What am I gonna do with you."

Jim enjoys seeing Joy this way. Dottie looks puzzled. Beth
is annoyed. Timmy takes a picture of his mom.

Oblivious to the others, Joy enjoys the music. Then she
lowers the volume. The music continues faintly.

                    JOY
          The thing about Smack Daddy is --

                    DOTTIE
          Who?

                    JOY
               (holds up Smack Daddy's debut
                CD)
          Smack Daddy.

                    JIM
          He - have I ever heard ...

                    TIMMY
          He's a black singer, Dad. You wouldn't
          know him.

Beth shoots a glare at Timmy.

                    TIMMY (cont'd)   *
          Well, it's true.

                    JOY
          May I finish?

                    JIM
          Please.

                                              (CONTINUED)

83   CONTINUED: 83

                              JOY
              The thing about Smack Daddy is: You know
              with him it's no one-night stand. That
              it's forever. Millions want him, but
              it's as if he's singing only to me, *baby*.
              Age doesn't matter - he doesn't care that
              I'm old and sick and falling apart - he
              sees my soul. He's not fickle ... he's
              there for me.

                              BETH
              Like Dad?

                              JOY
              Well, your father can't sing.

     Beat.

                              JOY (cont'd)
              But Smack Daddy. Oh man. He's got this
              secret little look when he's singing. He
              may not be that good looking, but man
              alive is he sexy.

     Beth sighs, unable to hide her exasperation.

                              JOY (cont'd)
              Which does lead to a whole sexual thing -
              I mean, it does bring up some kind of
              nice memories.

     Jim smiles.

                              BETH
              You mean, with like Dad, right?

                              JOY
              Him, too.

     Beat. Joy leans back and turns up the volume.

84   INT. APRIL'S APARTMENT - KITCHEN AREA   84

     April drops bite-sized chunks of sweet potatoes into a hot   *
     skillet. They *sizzle* slightly.

     There's a KNOCK at her door.   *

     As she pushes the chunks of sweet potato around using a
     spatula, she sprinkles brown sugar on them with her other
     hand ... until they caramelize.

                                                        (CONTINUED)

The KNOCKING persists.   *

April opens her door to find Wayne standing there, worried.   *

                    WAYNE   *
              (out of breath)   *
          Hello, I found you, it wasn't easy, I   *
          knocked on a lot of doors, but that's all   *
          right. Really it is.   *

April hurries back into the kitchen, letting the door go and   *
it closes on Wayne.   *

                    APRIL   *
              (all business)   *
          How's it going?   *

                    WAYNE   *
          No foreseeable problems.   *
              (pushing open the door, calling   *
               into the apartment)   *
          I was about to check your turkey myself,   *
          but then I thought since it's yours,   *
          maybe you'd prefer to do the checking.   *

                    APRIL
          OK.   *

                    WAYNE   *
          I certainly could do it for you. And   *
          will if you'd like. I didn't want to   *
          presume ...   *

                    APRIL   *
          Fine, whatever.   *

By now, Wayne is standing in April's kitchen.   *

                    WAYNE   *
          It's a common misconception that you can
          just stick a turkey in the oven.
              (beat)
          A turkey needs to be tended to, he needs
          to be cared for lovingly. One must pay
          close attention to poultry.

                    APRIL
              (trying not to laugh)
          Sure, OK...

                    WAYNE
          So much can go wrong. The turkey can dry   *
          out, burn in places; be overcooked;
                    (MORE)
                                              (CONTINUED)

84   CONTINUED: (2)   84

                              WAYNE (cont'd)   *
                    under-cooked, which is a health hazard;   *
                    and *what about basting?*

                              APRIL   *
                        (starting to get annoyed)   *
                    Look, Wayne, I'll be up in a second, OK?   *

Silence. Wayne stands there as April keeps working.   *

                              WAYNE   *
                    A second's up.   *

                              APRIL
                        (annoyed now)
                    Just give me a minute.   *

                              WAYNE   *
                    Sure.   *
                        (with humor)   *
                    Tick tock.   *

Wayne leaves.   *

Thinking Wayne is gone...   *

                              APRIL   *
                        (mocking)   *
                    Tick tock.   *

As April laughs to herself, we see Wayne watching, hurt, from   *
the hallway. He disappears from our view, then pulls the   *
door closed *hard.*   *

Startled, April turns in the direction of the door.

85   INT. HALLWAY OUTSIDE APARTMENT #30 - MOMENTS LATER   85   *

April climbs the last steps only to find ...

Wayne stuffing a "poop" bag in his coat pocket, about to
leave his apartment with Bernadette who pulls at her leash.

                              APRIL
                        (calling out)
                    Wait, here I am ...   *

                              WAYNE
                    No, I don't think so.   *

                              APRIL   *
                    What?   *

                                                          (CONTINUED)

85

                              WAYNE   *
                    We're going to have a mess on our hands   *
                    if I don't get Bernadette outside.   *

                              APRIL
                    Can I just pop my head in?   *

Wayne pulls the door closed.

                              APRIL (cont'd)
                    I'll be real quick.

                              WAYNE   *
                    I'm afraid not.   *

                              APRIL   *
                    I'll be real quick.   *

                              WAYNE   *
                    I don't think so.   *

Wayne takes out his keys.

                              APRIL   *
                    Come on, Wayne --

                              WAYNE
                    Do you know that good feeling that often
                    comes from being helpful?

                              APRIL
                    Yes?

                              WAYNE
                    I'm not having that feeling here.

Wayne locks the door.

                              APRIL
                    I didn't realize -- I'm sorry -- I got so
                    caught up in everything --

                              WAYNE
                    Do you know what they say about "sorry"?

                              APRIL
                    No.

                              WAYNE
                    It's just an excuse to do it again.
                         (beat)
                              (MORE)

                                                    (CONTINUED)

85   CONTINUED: (2)   85

                         WAYNE (cont'd)
               So I ask myself, "Wayne, it's very clear
               what you're doing for her. But what are
               you getting out of this?"

                         APRIL
                    (stumped)
               Well...

                         WAYNE
               I think you need to take some time and   *
               think about that. So that maybe later
               you help me understand what I'm getting
               from this exchange.
                    (under his breath)
               If we can even call it an exchange.
                    (starts toward the stairs)
               Come along, Bernadette.

          April watches as Wayne and his dog disappear down the stairs.

86   INT. GOODWILL - LATER THAT MORNING   86

          Near the cash register Latrell adjusts the picture on the
          small black and white TV he's plugged in. He's watching the
          Macy's Thanksgiving Day Parade.

          Bobby has been through racks of clothes, no luck. He's
          growing agitated. He holds up various outfits in the triple
          mirror of the Goodwill. He's trying to see how he'd look.

                         BOBBY
               Aw crap, Latrell.
                    (notices Latrell isn't
                     listening to him)
               Latrell!

          Latrell looks in Bobby's direction, smiles.

                         LATRELL
               Keep looking.

          Latrell returns to watching the TV.

          Beat as Bobby continues looking. He finds something, holds
          it up. It's an *all white leisure suit*.

                         BOBBY
               Oh, man, these are pimp clothes!

          Latrell laughs.

87   INT. GOODWILL - MINUTES MORNING   87

Latrell holds up a suit for Bobby.

                    BOBBY
          No.

He holds up a second suit.

                    BOBBY (cont'd)
          No!

He holds up a third, a fourth, a fifth.

                    BOBBY (cont'd)
          No! No! No!!!

88   INT. GOODWILL - MINUTES LATER   88

Bobby, exhausted, has given up. He sits dejected. Every
article of clothing has been looked over.

Latrell passes in front of Bobby, carrying a special pole (a
grabber).

Bobby looks up, sees ...

Latrell use the grabber to lower an old suit bag from the
highest rack.

Bobby watches.

Close on Latrell's fingers as they unzip the suit bag.

Close on Bobby's face as ...

Latrell removes an astonishing purple-black suit in
impeccable condition from the garment bag.

Bobby looks suddenly hopeful.

Quick shots of arms slipping into sleeves, legs into pants,
etc.

Camera pans up from his stocking feet, moving up his body to
his *disappointed* face. The suit is, quite simply, *too big*.

                    BOBBY
          Aw, crap.

                                              (CONTINUED)

                    LATRELL
          Not a problem, big man.

89   EXT. BURNS FAMILY CAR - INTERSTATE 280   89

In the back seat, Timmy's flipping the large photo album he's taken from his back pack.

Dottie looks over his shoulder. Beth refuses to look.

                    DOTTIE
          What do you have there?

                    TIMMY
          These are some photos of Mom ... I've
          taken, ever since ... you know.

                    DOTTIE
          How nice.

                    TIMMY
          I got a camera for my birthday.

                    JOY
          Timmy's very talented.

                    JIM
          All our children are talen--

                    JOY
          Yes, Beth's talented, too.

Close on the photos in the album. The first is a photo of a beaming Joy, healthy, with her real hair.

                    DOTTIE
          Oh, how nice.

                      JIM
          Maybe this isn't the best time...

Timmy looks at his mother, wondering if he should turn the page. Joy nods for him to continue.

Timmy turns the page. A tasteful shot of Joy with her top off, her breasts visible.

                    TIMMY
          That was before ... (her surgery).

                                    (CONTINUED)

                              JOY
                    So I could remember them always.

Dottie is understandably rattled.

                              JIM
                    OK, that's probably enough.

                              BETH
                    I think so.

                              JOY
                    Keep going, Timmy.

Timmy turns the pages quickly. We get only glimpses of
candid shots of Joy.

                              JOY (cont'd)
                    Stop.

Timmy stops.

                              JOY (cont'd)
                    This is my favorite.

It's a close up of a post-operative mastectomy scar. Bright
sunlight pours in the background of the photograph.

                              JOY (cont'd)
                    Look at the light in this one. The
                    angle, too. And the colors ...

                              DOTTIE
                    I think I prefer Beth's singing.

Beat. Timmy closes the photo album.

90   INT. APRIL'S APARTMENT -- HALLWAY   90

Quick cuts:

April opens a can of cream of mushroom soup for the green
bean casserole.

She opens a can of french fried onions.

Empty cans tossed into the plastic trash can.

April unfolds two card tables, sets them next to each other,
they're unequal heights.

                                        (CONTINUED)

90   CONTINUED: 90

She tries to make them level by sliding cut pieces of
cardboard under the legs of the shorter table.

She covers the table with a patterned paper table cloth.

She sets a stack of plates on the table, and the table
wobbles. In the hallway, a NOISE can be heard. April lunges
toward the door.

91   INT. HALLWAY OUTSIDE APRIL'S APARTMENT   91

April stands in the doorway of her apartment.

                    APRIL
          Wayne?

Wayne isn't there.

92   EXT. APARTMENT HALLWAY - MOMENTS LATER   92

April brings out a garbage bag full of balloons, packets of
streamers, tape, scissors, and begins to decorate the
hallway.

93   INT. GOODWILL STORE - DAY   93

Bobby stands on a chair, wearing the baggy suit. Latrell
uses straight pins to shorten the cuffs on the suit coat.

                    LATRELL
          You ever hear the phrase: Beware the
          occasion that warrants a new suit.

                    BOBBY
          No.   *

                    LATRELL
          I'm tellin' ya -- Beware.

                    BOBBY
          Well, you ever been in love?   *

                    LATRELL
          Not interested.

                    BOBBY
          It does things to you.

                                              (CONTINUED)

                    LATRELL
          Don't move.

                    BOBBY
          You do things you don't think you'd ever
          or could ever do. My mama, god rest her
          soul ...

                    LATRELL
          Not a mama story.

                    BOBBY
          No, she was driving ...

                    LATRELL
          Your mama didn't drive.

                    BOBBY
          You didn't know my mama, and I pity you
          for that.

                    LATRELL
          Don't pity me, big man.

                    BOBBY
          My mama was driving in Jamaica, and I was
          just a baby, and the car flipped over,
          and I was trapped under the car. And
          what did she do?
               (beat)
          She lifted up the car ...

                    LATRELL
          Bullshit.

                    BOBBY
          She lifted up the car and pulled me to
          safety.

                    LATRELL
          It's not possible.

                    BOBBY
          But she did it. She had this moment of
          unbelievable strength because she had
          love.

                    LATRELL
          Yeah, right.

                    BOBBY
          Latrell, that's what love does--

Bobby gets stuck with a pin.

> BOBBY (cont'd)   *
> Ouch.

> LATRELL
> You moved. I told you not to move.

94   INT. APRIL'S APARTMENT - KITCHEN AREA   94

April enters the apartment from having decorated the hallway.
We see the table needs to be set, leftover decorations cover
one of the card tables. Recipe books are out, boxes of food
and jars of spices crowd her one small counter. April
doesn't know what to do next.

95   EXT. HIGHWAY - EAST TO NEW YORK CITY   95

The Burns family car winds down the last hilly, bucolic road
in New Jersey.

We hear the faint sound of a Woman (Beth) singing an operatic
ballad in Italian.

96   INT. BURNS FAMILY CAR   96

The final notes of Beth's aria.

A note about Beth's singing voice: She is an excellent
singer, with beautiful tone, near perfect pitch, with only
one draw back: she tends to over-enunciate her words.

She hits one last high note.

Close up shots of ...

Jim, pleased.

Dottie, pleased.

Timmy, focusing his camera on Beth.

Joy, holding her head, moaning softly.

Beth finishes, Dottie claps, Jim whistles.

(CONTINUED)

> DOTTIE
> Bravo.

> JIM
> Encore, Encore!

> BETH
> Any requests?

> JOY
> That you stop.

Beat. Beth is stunned by what Joy said, as if the wind had been knocked out of her.

> JOY (cont'd)
> (not really meaning it)
> I'm sorry.   That was ... terrible.

Beat as big tears begin to roll down Beth's face.

Dottie leans forward to get a better look at Joy. To avoid her mother's staring, Joy looks out the window.

> DOTTIE
> (beat)
> Who are you?

> JOY
> Don't start with that. You know who I am.

> DOTTIE
> I know who you *say* you are. But my daughter is kind, and sweet, and soft spoken ...

> JOY
> Not anymore.

> DOTTIE
> Then I don't know you.

97 INT. GAS STATION BATHROOM   97

Joy, on her knees, bent over the toilet. She dips out of view and vomits.

(CONTINUED)

> JOY (O.S.)
> Aw, fuck.

CUT TO:

Close on Gas Station sink. Joy's hands wash out an edge
section of her wig.

> JIM (O.S.)
> Joy, you all right?

Wide Shot - a glimpse of Joy, bald, putting on her wig.

98   EXT. GAS STATION DOOR - MOMENTS LATER   98

Joy opens the door, smiles. Her eyes red from crying.

99   EXT. BURNS FAMILY CAR - MINUTES LATER   99

The Burns Family car is back on the highway, heading toward
Manhattan.

> JOY
> I am so critical. It's one of my worst
> faults. Some of the reasons for this are
> obvious. But, why, I keep asking myself,
> why have I been so hard, for instance, on
> you, Beth, when for years you've been the
> daughter of my dreams? You have. You
> know you have. Apart from your weight
> problems, we're practically the same
> person. So why am I so hard on you?
> Forget the fact you're making the same
> mistakes I made, and I wish you'd make
> your own, I think I'm hard on you because
> we've had so many good times. And I
> think it's likely as this gets worse,
> Timmy, I'll be hard on you, too, because
> we've had so many good times. So why
> then am I so hard on April, when we
> didn't have that many good times ...

> JIM
> That's not true --

(CONTINUED)

                    JOY
        For days I've been trying to think of
        nice April memories, and I could only
        come up with one. One vivid, beautiful
        memory. But there's gotta be more ...

                    DOTTIE
        One can be a lot.

                    JIM
        What was it?

                    JOY
        It's not important -

                    JIM
        Like hell it isn't. Tell us.

                    JOY
        OK. She had just turned three. She's   *
        looking out the picture window on Locust
        Street - it was early in the morning, but
        it was already sunny - she was just
        gazing out the window and she turned back
        to me and said, "Oh, Mother, don't you
        just love every day?"

Beat as Joy savors the memory.

                    BETH
        That was me.
            (beat)
        It was. April was six when we lived on   *
        Locust Street.   *

                    JOY
        Is that right?

An awkward beat as Beth is right.

                    JIM
        Well, what about that crayon drawing she
        made of the Mayflower, the one you had
        framed --

                    BETH
        That was me, too.

Timmy glares at Beth.

                    BETH (CONT'D) (cont'd)
        Sorry. It's important that we're
        accurate. They're my memories too.

                                        (CONTINUED)

                    JOY
        You're absolutely right, god fucking
        dammit.

                    JIM
        Just off the top of my head, I have one.
        She was, I don't how old, but she was
        wearing a pink nightgown -

                    TIMMY
        That was me.
            (beat)
        Kidding.

                    BETH
        Ha, ha.

                    JIM
        I'd been on a trip, or maybe not, but I
        came into her room, and she was in her
        crib. She was sleeping. It was lovely.

                    TIMMY
        That's it?

                    JOY
        Yep.

                    DOTTIE
        That's lovely.

                    JOY
        No, it's not. Your happiest memory, she
        was asleep!

                    JIM
            (laughing)
        I didn't say it was my happiest. It's
        just what came to mind.

100   EXT. SIDE OF ROAD   100

        The Burns car has pulled off the road and stopped suddenly.
        Joy's door swings open and Joy bolts from the car.

        Beat. Inside the car no one moves.

                    TIMMY
        Who's going to get her this time -

        Jim is already out his door.

                                        (CONTINUED)

Angle on:

Joy crossing the barren two lane highway. She is walking in
the opposite direction.

                    JIM
          What are you doing?

Joy holds up a thumb to catch a ride from a passing car.

                    JOY
          No. It's shitty, Jim. All I remember is
          the petulance, the shop lifting, the fire
          in the kitchen ...

                    JIM
          Which was an accident.

                    JOY
          Was it an accident the way she used to
          light matches and throw them at Beth? Or
          that time she used a lighter to cut
          Timmy's bangs?

                    JIM
          Joy ...

                    JOY
          The drugs. The ingratitude. She bit my
          nipples whenever I tried to breast feed.

                    JIM
          Sweetie, come on -

                    JOY
          No wonder there's cancer! *She's* the
          cancer.

Joy moves down the road, out of frame.

                    JIM
          Joy, get back in the ...   *

                                                                *

101   INT. BURNS FAMILY CAR - SIDE OF ROAD - CONTINUOUS   101

          Timmy, Beth and Dottie watch from inside the car.

                    DOTTIE
          What's going on?

(CONTINUED)

101   CONTINUED: 101

                         TIMMY
                    (beat)
               Mom needed to stretch her legs.

Beth sighs in disgust at Timmy's explanation.

102   EXT. SIDE OF ROAD   102

Jim continues to pursue Joy.

                         JOY
               I tried, OK? But I can't go. I can't -
               I can't take another bad experience with
               her ...

                         JIM
               But it won't be like that.

                         JOY
               You don't know that.

                         JIM
               It's the whole point of going. We're
               making a memory.

                         JOY
               You're not listening to me. I have too
               many memories ...

                         JIM
               A *good* memory. We're making something
               good.

                         JOY
               What if it's not!

                         JIM
               It will be, I promise. It will be
               beautiful.

                         JOY
                    (Drops her outstretched
                    hitchhiker's thumb)
               How do you know?

                         JIM
               Because I told her it had to be.

                         JOY
                    (Beat, surrender)
               And if it's not?

                                             (CONTINUED)

102 CONTINUED: 102

                              JIM
                     (holds Joy, smiles)
                  Then I'll kill her.

     Beat as we stay on Jim holding Joy. Then ...

103 INT. OUTSIDE OF APARTMENT #30   103

     April, panicked, knocks on the door.

                              APRIL
                  Are you back yet? Wayne, are you there?
                  Wayne?
                         (pounding on door)
                  Wayne!!!

104 INT. APRIL'S APARTMENT   104

     Camera pans throughout April's apartment. Mess,
     disorganization everywhere.

     We hear April on the phone before we see her:

                              APRIL
                  I'd like to report a ...

                              DISPATCHER (O.S.)
                  Ma'am, you need to speak up.

                              APRIL
                  ... a *kidnapping*... this man ...

                              DISPATCHER (O.S.)
                  Try to calm down, speak slowly.

                              APRIL
                  This *creepy* man has taken my turkey
                  hostage ... and he's been gone now ...

                              DISPATCHER (O.S.)
                  Did you say "turkey"?

                              APRIL
                  Yes, that piece of creepy shit has my
                  turkey!

                              DISPATCHER (O.S.)
                  911 is strictly for emergencies --

                                                          (CONTINUED)

                              APRIL
                I know that! That's what this is --

The sound of the other line HANGING UP.

April slams down the phone.

Beat. She thinks. Then she moves about frantically opening
drawers, etc., looking for a pen or pencil. She finally
finds a Magic Marker.

Crossing the room, she stops before the much revised note
she'd left for Bobby.

Close on April's note to Bobby as April writes in emphatic
block print:

                    WHERE ARE YOU!?!?!

105   OMITTED   105   *

105A EXT. STREETS OF NEW YORK CITY   105A   *

      Shots of Bobby traveling downtown on his scooter, standing   *
      proud in his new suit.   *
                                                                   *

106   OMITTED   106   *

                                                             *

107   INT. APRIL'S APARTMENT   107

      April lifts up her apartment window. She crawls out on the
      back fire escape, carrying a small crow bar.

108   EXT. BACK OF APRIL'S APARTMENT BUILDING -- FIRE ESCAPE   108

      As quickly as she can, April climbs the three flights of the
      black wrought-iron fire escape.

109   EXT. FIFTH FLOOR FIRE ESCAPE -- CONTINUOUS   109

      April stops outside Wayne's Window.

                                              (CONTINUED)

April's POV: Wayne's Apartment. Most of the apartment is
pitch black, except for, in the distance, a faint glow from
Wayne's kitchen, where his brand new oven stands *gleaming*.

April tries to lift the window, but it's locked. She tries a
second window, it's *not* locked. But it's stuck. She uses
the crowbar to loosen the window frame. Then, up goes the
window.

Just as she's about to climb in, a dog GROWLS.

April looks up.

Wayne is standing there, petting a snarling Bernadette.

April gasps, falls back.

                    WAYNE
              (glaring, said to April)
         Bad girl.

Before April can collect herself to respond, Wayne slams shut
the window and yanks down the shade.

110   INT. HALLWAY OUTSIDE OF APARTMENT #30   110

We follow behind April who climbs the last steps only to find
Wayne standing in his doorway, waiting with a smug smile.

                    WAYNE
         So this is the thanks I get...

                    APRIL
         I want my turkey.

                    WAYNE
         After all I've done for you.

                    APRIL
         I want it now.

                    WAYNE
         I was afraid it would come to this --

                    APRIL
         Give me my turkey!

                    WAYNE
         I'm looking for a word.

                                            (CONTINUED)

                         APRIL
          Give me my mother-fucking bird, *please*!

                         WAYNE
          Ah, that's better.
               (stepping out of the way)
          She's all yours.

April blows past Wayne into his apartment. During the
following, she pulls down the oven door, grabs the hot pads,
lifts out the turkey, and starts to leave.

                         WAYNE (cont'd)
          You don't have to thank me.

                         APRIL
          Don't worry.

                         WAYNE
          Thank Bernadette.

                         APRIL
          What?

                         WAYNE
          Without her, we wouldn't have found a
          solution.

Out in the hallway now, April turns back. What is he talking
about? For the first time, she looks down at her turkey.

                         WAYNE (cont'd)
          She prefers her meat lightly fried.

At the stove, Wayne takes a lid off a skillet and lifts up *a
large turkey leg.* He holds it above Bernadette who yelps and
jumps for it.

                         WAYNE (cont'd)
               (as if talking to a baby)
          Would sweetie like it cut into little
          pieces?

April starts *shrieking.* Wayne starts to close the door with
his available hand, but April lunges toward the door and
blocks it from closing all the way. A brief struggle, and
April pushes her way inside, the door closes. We hear the
sound of violence coming from the other side of the door.

111   INT. STAIRWELL - MINUTES LATER   111

An empty stairwell.

We hear the sound of the door open. Heavy breathing.

Silence.

We see her feet first, then her legs, then her turkey --
missing a leg -- which she carries. April, near tears, is
descending the stairs.

Halfway down the flight of steps, she sits down. We see in
her hand she's also holding *Wayne's TOUPEE.*

                    WAYNE (O.S.)
          You're a bad girl. A bad, *bad* girl. A
          very bad ...

                    APRIL
              (faintly)
          No, I'm not.

The sound of DOG PAWS running across the floor. Bernadette
appears above April on the top step. She waits, panting
loudly.

Without looking back, April tosses the toupee behind her.
Bernadette picks it up in her mouth and scampers back to
Wayne. The door shuts, locks turn.

Angle on:

LEE QUONG, age 7, and his sister, LEE LANG, age 10, watch
from around the corner. They disappear.

Close on April. She covers her face with her hands. Behind
her, a MAN (we only see his legs) approaches.

The Man reaches out his hand and gently touches her on the
shoulder.

Startled, April jumps up, turns around, sees ...

LEE KAI, the father. He's a man in his mid-fifties.
Standing behind him are his two children, and the rest of the
Lee family, recent emigres from Northern China: LEE WAI YAM,
the mother, LEE GUONG TAN, the grandmother, and LEE LOUNG
CHI, the bachelor uncle, all staring, concerned.

April lets out a cry so loud that it's almost comical.

112   INT. LEE FAMILY STUDIO APARTMENT -- MOMENTS LATER   112

As April is led into the room, carrying the turkey pan, we
see...

One room, where the entire family lives. A set of bunk beds.
A standing coat rack. Suitcases used like closets. A very,
very good TV with a VCD (Chinese version of DVD) presently
playing Chinese language disc.   A small altar -- where
incense is often burned -- with a small ivory Chinese
figurine with a framed black and white photo of the deceased
grandfather.

As the Uncle turns off the large TV, or at least turns the
volume down, April looks around the room, afraid to trust
that she's in a safe place.

The Mother gestures for April to sit, which she does.

April stares at the stove, identical to the one in April's
apartment. She's speechless.

The Mother and the Grandmother gently take the turkey pan
from April's mitted hands. They speak softly to each other
in Chinese.

The Grandmother and Mother empty the stove, which is full of
the families most precious belongings all packed in Danish
butter cookie tins. Also, several pairs of colorful, hand-
sewn Chinese slippers are removed.

The Daughter brings a warm wet cloth for April to wash her
face.

The Uncle offers her a drink of brandy.

April shakes her head "No."

The Son brings out a large bottle of Sprite.

April nods "Yes."

She's handed a plastic cup. The Son pours the Sprite into
April's cup.

The stove is turned on, the gas catches ...

And April takes a sip.

113   EXT. STREETS OF LOWER EAST SIDE - OUTSIDE BODEGA   113   *

Bobby emerges with three bunches of flowers.   *

He's about to start his scooter when an OLDER WOMAN passes   *
and smiles her approval.   *

                    OLDER WOMAN
          Now don't you look nice ...

Bobby smiles as the Older Woman walks on.   *

Behind him, a LARGE SHADOW casts itself over the scene.

                    LARGE SHADOW
          Now don't you look nice.

Startled, Bobby turns, sees the source of the shadow.

A SKINNY WHITE GUY, with a jagged scar on his left cheek and
a gold tooth, wearing baggy clothes. His hair hasn't been
combed in weeks, as he's trying to grow dreadlocks. The
Skinny White guy is best described as a home boy wannabe.

                    SKINNY WHITE GUY
          How ya been, Bobby?

                    BOBBY
          Do I know you?

                    SKINNY WHITE GUY
          Do you know me? You only ruined my life.

                    BOBBY
          I'm sorry?

                    SKINNY WHITE GUY
          She was mine first.

                    BOBBY
          Eddie?
              (fights laughing)
          You're Eddie?

                    SKINNY WHITE GUY
          Eddie died when she dumped me. Now I'm
          Tyrone.

                    BOBBY
          Oh, well, it's nice to finally meet you.

                                                        (CONTINUED)

                    TYRONE
             (a wreck)
I changed my name. Seeing that everybody
else is changing, the whole world
changing, my whole world which was
April...

                    BOBBY
Whatever, I gotta get --

                    TYRONE
             (indicating the suit)
You must be doing good.

                    BOBBY
Not in the way you think.

                    TYRONE
Well, what am I thinking?

                    BOBBY
I wouldn't know.

                    TYRONE
             (smiling)
Even if I wanted to hurt you, and I kind
of do, I won't.

                    BOBBY
Oh.
             (mock relieved)
Whew.

                    TYRONE
So you can relax.

                    BOBBY
Thanks.

                    TYRONE
It's her choice. I mean, she wants to be
with you, fine. It's just ... there's
something I'd like to ...
             (beginning to cry)
If you could *tell* her ... something for
me ...

                    BOBBY
What do you want me to tell her?

Tyrone steps toward Bobby with his arms outstretched. Bobby
doesn't know what to do. Tyrone hugs him, stretches up to
whisper in Bobby's ear:

                                          (CONTINUED)

                         TYRONE
                     (with menace)
                  Happy Thanksgiving.

Several YOUNG PUNKS on bicycles arrive behind Tyrone. These
punks seem to represent every nationality imaginable. They
are the United Colors of Benetton of Young Punks.

At first Bobby laughs. Then Bobby runs.

                                        SMASH CUT TO:

114   EXT. STREETS OF LOWER EAST SIDE   114

Bobby runs down an alley. Behind him, we hear the whoops and
hollers of the Young Punks pursuing him.

115   INT. LEE FAMILY STUDIO APARTMENT -- LATER   115

April's hands touch the door of the Lee family oven. She
feels the warmth.

As April speaks the following, Lee Lang, the daughter,
translates in Chinese for the rest of the family.

                         APRIL
                  Once there were people here called
                  Indians. Native Americans. Whatever.
                  Then a boat came called the Mayflower and
                  it landed on a big rock carrying people
                  like me. The first year on their own was
                  hard ...
                     (getting emotional)
                  Really, really hard ...
                     (beat)
                  Let me start again --

116   EXT. STREETS OF LOWER EAST SIDE   116

Bobby scales a chain link fence and drops over the other
side.

The chingy rattle sound of the Young Punks grasping the chain
link fence!

117   INT. LEE FAMILY STUDIO APARTMENT -- MOMENTS LATER   117

April tries again. Shots of the faces of the family members
as they listen. Lee Lang continues to translate.

                    APRIL
            (sweetly, for them)
    This was long ago, before we stole their
    land, and killed most of them, and moved
    the rest to reservations --
    before they lost their language and their
    customs ...
        (realizing who she's talking
         to)
    OK, forget what I just said --

118   EXT. STREETS OF LOWER EAST SIDE   118

The Young Punks chasing Bobby ride past a dumpster.

Another angle:

Bobby lies inside the dumpster, amongst the garbage, waiting
for them to pass.

119   INT. LEE FAMILY STUDIO APARTMENT -- MOMENTS LATER   119

April is still struggling to explain.

                    APRIL
    OK, OK! Once there was this one day
    where everybody seemed to know they
    needed each other ...
     This one day when they knew for certain
    they couldn't do it alone. And so ...

Beat. April looks around at them, unable to find other
words, as Lee Lang finishes translating for the rest of the
family.

120   EXT. STREET OF LOWER EAST SIDE - BACK ALLEY   120

Bobby drops to the ground from the dumpster. He turns, stops
when he sees...

Tyrone and the Young Punks block his only escape.

                                        (CONTINUED)

120   CONTINUED: 120

Close on Bobby, breathing heavily, waiting for what will come
next.

                                        SCREEN TO BLACK:

121   EXT. BURNS CAR IN THE HOLLAND TUNNEL   121

The darkness of the Holland Tunnel breaks as the Burns family
car emerges into Lower Manhattan.

Jim glances over and sees ...

Joy. Her eyes closed, her mouth slightly open, slack jawed,
her head resting against the window.

                    JIM
            Oh, god.

Jim pulls the car over.

                    BETH
            No, Daddy, she's asleep ...

                    JIM
            I thought ...

                    BETH
            She's *sleeping*.

Jim throws the car in park. He covers his face with his
hands.

                    JOY
            (waking, sees Jim, then softly)
            Aw, Jimmy ...

122   EXT. MANHATTAN ENTRANCE TO HOLLAND TUNNEL   122

The Burns family car sits idle on the side of the road, as
all other traffic rushes past in both directions.

123   MONTAGE OF APRIL DOING TASKS   123

Culminating with April rescuing the turkey-shaped Salt and
Pepper shakers from the trash.

124   OMITTED   124   *

                                                                  *

125   OMITTED   125   *

                                                                  *

126   EXT.   STREETS OF LOWER MANHATTAN   126

The Burns family car drives through the streets of the Lower
East Side.

Jim is alert at the wheel, overly cautious. The others look
for street signs. Beth reads out instructions. Joy stares
out the window at the various people on the street.

                    BETH
               (looking at street sign in
                distance)
          Avenue ... C ...
               (checks sheet)
          We're looking for D. So maybe turn
          up ...

The Street Light turns from Green to Yellow ...

Jim accelerates to make the light, then suddenly slams on the
brakes, nearly hitting ...

THE GANG OF YOUNG PUNKS on small bicycles (the same ones we
saw before, except they have cuts and scrapes on their faces,
from their fight with Bobby) ...

                    JIM (O.S.)
          Damn!

The Young Punks on the Bikes circle the Burns family car,
making it impossible for them to move. We hear the FAMILIAR   *
DRONE of Bobby's scooter. One of the Punks is riding it.   *

                    PUNK ON BIKE
               (calling back)
          Look where you're going next time, Mother
          Fucker!

POV from inside the car: The Young Punks circle for a few
moments, there's an opening, Jim hits the gas, speeds off
nearly crashing into a taxi.

                                                      (CONTINUED)

126 CONTINUED: 126

                              BETH (O.S.)
                    No, Dad. You missed the turn!

127 INT. APRIL'S APARTMENT   127

April stirs a small pot on the stove.

A KNOCK on her door.

April looks up, freezes, goes to door and opens it.

Lee Lang stands with her brother Lee Quong.

                              APRIL
                    Yes?   *

128 INT. STAIRWELL OF APRIL'S BUILDING - MOMENTS LATER   128

April quickly follows Lee Lang and Lee Quong up the stairs.

129 INT. APRIL'S APARTMENT - KITCHEN AREA   129

Close on the small pan on the burner, the lid lifts slightly
as the sauce begins to boil.

130 INT. THE LEE APARTMENT   130

April watches as the turkey bag is cut away from the turkey.

The turkey is golden brown, thoroughly cooked, with one added
feature: *It has both legs.*

April stares at it in disbelief.

                              APRIL
                    I don't understand. How did ...?

                              LEE WAI YAM (THE MOTHER)
                    Sick jai.

                              APRIL
                    What?

                              LEE WAI YAM (THE MOTHER)
                    Sick jai.

                                                     (CONTINUED)

130   CONTINUED: 130

                         LEE LANG (THE DAUGHTER)
                           (translating)
                    Sick jai is carved Tofu.

April gestures speechlessly. A miracle.   *

131   EXT. APRIL'S STREET   131

POV from inside moving car: Trash. Bodega with Rusty Gates.
The Abandoned Building. The Empty Lot with garbage in it.
Homeless man asleep on cardboard box, with grocery cart
beside him, full of cans.

                         DOTTIE
                    Oh my.

                         BETH
                    Oh my god.

                         JIM
                    This must be the wrong street.

POV from inside car as it comes to a stop: The front door of
April's building is decorated with a colorful turkey made out
of construction paper. The sign reads, "Welcome."

                         TIMMY
                    No, I think we're here.

                         JIM
                           (upset)
                    No, no. It can't be. This isn't it.
                           (snatches paper with address on
                            it from Beth)
                    We've obviously got the wrong ...

                         BETH
                    Daddy, I think this is it.

Jim puts the car in park. He turns off the engine.

                         JIM
                           (under his breath)
                    Dammit, April.

POV from Inside Car: A black man in a torn suit, his
forehead and lip cut, approaches the car.   *

                         JIM (cont'd)
                    Lock your doors.

                                              (CONTINUED)

> BOBBY
> Welcome, welcome.   Hi!   You made it.
> Good.
> > (awkward beat)
> You're April's family, aren't you?

No one answers. Joy lowers her window.

> BOBBY (cont'd)
> Hi. You're her mother.
> > (awkward beat)
> I'm... just a friend.
> > (hesitates)
> That's not true. I'm Bobby. *The* Bobby
> who loves your daughter. The Bobby who
> would do anything for her.

The family members, even Timmy, look mortified. But not Joy.
She's staring at Bobby, and to her surprise, she finds him
rather endearing.

> BOBBY (cont'd)
> > (looking at Joy)
> Uhm -- the Bobby who normally doesn't
> look like this.

Jim pushes the electric window button to close Joy's window.

> BOBBY (cont'd)
> How about if I --
> Why don't I just go get her?

As Joy's window closes, we hear Beth blurt out: "Oh my God."
The rest of the family, except Joy, begin talking all at
once.

Angle from outside the car: Joy stares at Bobby, smiling
slightly. We see Bobby's reflection in the window. He
smiles, turns and disappears into the building.

132   INT. APRIL'S BUILDING - STAIRWELL - DAY   132

As April carries the finished turkey down the stairs, Bobby
races up the stairs. They call to each other, meeting just
outside April's apartment. April sees his face and clothes
and before she can ask, Bobby says:

                                                        (CONTINUED)

                         BOBBY
                    (out of breath)
                  They're here!

133   INT. APRIL'S APARTMENT   133

Close on the Pot. It's *bubbling over.* We hear the locks
turning, the door opens.

                         APRIL
                    (as she rushes in)
                  What happened--

                         BOBBY
                    (also frantic)
                  I'll tell you later --

                         APRIL
                    (removing the pan from the
                     stove)
                  But Bobby --

                         BOBBY
                  You got to go.

During the following, they move about frantically - Bobby
taking care of the flowers and the pan on the stove. April
checking herself in the mirror and getting Bobby a Band-Aid.
Somehow they end up kissing each other in between their words
spoken excitedly, nervously, quickly.

                         APRIL
                  You alright?

                         BOBBY
                  Yes.

April opens a cabinet.

                         BOBBY (cont'd)
                  I'll take care of everything.

                         APRIL
                    (touched)
                  You got flowers.

                         BOBBY
                  I'll take care of them. What are you
                  doing?

                                              (CONTINUED)

133   CONTINUED: 133

                APRIL
            (looking for Band-Aids)
You need first aid.

                BOBBY
Just go.

                APRIL
I missed you.

                BOBBY
Oh, baby, I missed you. Go.

                APRIL
Wish me luck.

                BOBBY
You look great. Go.

                APRIL
Yes.
            (as she exits)
I'm gone!

134   INT. HALLWAY/STAIRWAY IN APRIL'S BUILDING   134

As April bounds down the stairs, we see the extensive
decorating job she's done -- streamers on the railing,
balloons spaced evenly all the way down.

As she passes the second floor, Evette is opening her door.

                EVETTE
We finished the cranberry --

                APRIL
            (not even hearing Evette, and
            not stopping to talk)
They're here! They're here!

April turns the corner, descends the last flight of steps,
pushes open the grey metal door and steps out onto...

135   EXT. APRIL'S STREET - CONTINUOUS   135

The empty street. April looks around. It's eerily quiet.
April stands there in disbelief as it sinks in.

136   EXT. FAMILY CAR - STREETS OF LOWER NEW YORK   136

The Burns family in their car. Silence as Jim drives.

                    JIM
              (boiling mad, said softly)
          We won't talk about her again.
              (beat)
          It was my mistake.
              (beat)
          I don't know what the hell I was
          thinking.

Silence.

                    JOY
              (heartbroken)
          So now what?

137   EXT. STREETS OF THE LOWER WEST SIDE   137

The Burns Car heads toward the Holland Tunnel.

138   INT. APRIL'S APARTMENT - DAY   138

Bobby stuffs his torn suit in the closet. He's trying to
dress (in a simple black shirt and black jeans) while he
arranges the flowers. He stops when he hears ...

A loud BANG, like a gunshot.

He goes out to the hallway, looks down the stairs.

Another BANG.

April is slowly walking up the stairs, popping each
decorative balloon she passes along the way.

The third BANG comes as we watch from Bobby's POV as she pops
yet another balloon.

139   INT. APRIL'S APARTMENT - MINUTES LATER   139

April dresses Bobby's cut on his forehead. She uses a large
white bandage which she cuts out using scissors. In between
"doctoring" Bobby, she uses the backs of her hands to wipe
away the tears which roll freely down her face.

                                              (CONTINUED)

139   CONTINUED: 139

                         BOBBY
          I mean, I don't understand -- they were
          just there. I saw them -- it's just --
          well, maybe, they ran an errand...?

                         APRIL
          Shhhh.

                         BOBBY
          Why would they come all this way?

     April lightly covers Bobby's mouth with her hand. She kisses
     where the bandage is on his forehead. She leaves the room,
     leaving Bobby stuck in mid-thought.

140   INT. APRIL'S BEDROOM - CONTINUOUS   140

     April, still dressed, crawls onto her bed.

     Bobby watches from the doorway, not knowing what to do as
     April cries. Then he gets down on the bed and *holds* her. He
     says "Shh" and "It's OK" and "I'm sorry" and he strokes her
     hair, but mostly he just holds her.

                         APRIL
                    (still crying)
          I knew it. I knew it.

     And it takes awhile, but finally April's crying slows down
     enough so she's able to ask:

                         APRIL (cont'd)
          What - are we gonna - do - with all the
          food?

141   EXT. NEW JERSEY DINER - PARKING LOT   141

     To establish. A big blue semi-truck pulls into view. The
     Burns family are already inside.

                         BETH (O.S.)
          Look at these prices.

142   INT. NEW JERSEY DINER   142

     Beth studies a menu. Jim sits next to her. Timmy, Joy and
     Dottie sit across from them. Joy is distracted.

                                                       (CONTINUED)

142   CONTINUED:

                    BETH
          You can't beat these prices and there's
          something for everyone.

Joy suddenly starts to stand.

                    JIM
          Joy? You OK?

                    JOY
          I need to use the bathroom.

                    BETH
          I'll come --

                    JOY
          No, Timmy can help me.

Timmy escorts Joy to the bathroom.

                    BETH
               (to Jim, thinking they're
               alone)
          Don't be hard on yourself. You did the
          right thing.

Angle on:

Joy is looking back toward the table.

                    BETH (O.S.) (cont'd)
          It's much better this way.

                    WAITRESS (O.S.)
          Good afternoon. Happy Thanksgiving.

143   INT. DINER BATHROOM   143

At the bathroom sink, Joy splashes water on her face. As she
looks at herself in the mirror, she overhears a YOUNG MOTHER
talking sternly to her YOUNG DAUGHTER.

                    YOUNG MOTHER
          I'm sick of your behavior. Sick and
          tired of it. I'm leaving now.

                    YOUNG GIRL
          But Mommy ...

                                          (CONTINUED)

143   CONTINUED:

>   YOUNG MOTHER
>   No, I'm *going*. And you're on your own.
>   We'll see how you like that.

The Young Mother emerges from the stall, doesn't even look at
Joy as she exits the bathroom.

Joy turns off the water from the sink faucet. She moves so
that she can see the Young Girl (10) in the reflection.

The Young Girl is upset and seems frozen with fear. She
stares at Joy.

Joy is about to say something when the Young Girl bolts and
runs out of the bathroom.

Beat. Joy looks at herself in the mirror.

144   INT. OUTSIDE OF BATHROOM - MOMENTS LATER   144

Determined, Joy blows past Timmy, moves through the diner...

>   TIMMY
>   Mom? You OK?

Joy's POV: Customers, the clinking of glass and silver,
people eating. A MEMBER OF A MOTORCYCLE GANG pays his bill   *
at the cash register.

Joy taps the MOTORCYCLE GANG MEMBER on the shoulder, and he   *
turns.

>   JOY
>   Is one of those yours?

145   INT. DINER - MOMENTS LATER   145

The Waitress recites the Specials of the Day for Beth, Jim,
and Dottie.

>   WAITRESS
>   Today only we're serving our world famous
>   giblet gravy. We've also got roast ham
>   for those who don't enjoy turkey. We've
>   got an all-you-can-eat buffet ...

                                                      (CONTINUED)

145   CONTINUED: 145

     Dottie's POV: Beth, Dottie and Jim are focused intently on   *
the waitress. Outside, the biker helps Joy strap on a   *
helmet. ANOTHER BIKER helps Timmy do the same.   *

146   EXT. NEW JERSEY DINER - PARKING LOT - CONTINUOUS   146

     As Joy gets situated on back of one motorcycle, Timmy climbs   *
on back of the second.   *

                      JOY
                   (shouting)   *
         What's your name?   *

147   EXT. NEW JERSEY HIGHWAY   147   *

     Joy and Timmy hold on as the motorcycles race off.   *

148   INT. NEW JERSEY DINER - LATER   148

     Jim, Beth and Dottie sit quietly, waiting for Joy and Timmy.
Their food has been served.

                      JIM   *
            I'm sure they'll be (right out)...

                    BETH   *
             (touching her plate)
           It's getting cold.

                      JIM
           Beth --

                    BETH
           I think I'll go check ...

149   EXT. APRIL'S STREET - DAY   149

     The two motorcycles pull up in front of April's building   *
carrying Joy & Timmy.   *

150   EXT. THE STREET OUTSIDE APRIL'S APARTMENT BUILDING   150   *

The biker helps Joy as she carefully climbs off the   *
motorcycle. He lifts her down.   *

Timmy waits with his camera ready. They pose for a picture
which Timmy takes.

                         JOY   *
              Thank you, Izzy.

                         IZZY   *
              Good luck.

                         JOY
              You, too.

Timmy holds the door to the vestibule open for Joy, who is
very weak and having trouble walking.

The Truck Driver watches this, then says:

                         IZZY   *
              May I?

Izzy easily, gently scoops her up.   *

                         JOY
                    (weakly, playfully)
              Well, Izzy, if I were any younger, you   *
              would not be safe.

Izzy starts up the stairs, cradling her in his arms.   *

151   INT. APRIL'S APARTMENT - DAY   151

Bobby helps April carve the turkey. She holds up a plate and
he serves a slice of turkey. April holds up a second plate.

There's a KNOCK ON THE DOOR.

As April crosses to answer the door, we see that the entire
Lee family is sitting around the dining room table, all
waiting to begin eating their first Thanksgiving meal.

April sets down two plates of turkey, both for the Lee
children, then she heads to the door ...

152   INT. OUTSIDE APRIL'S APARTMENT - CONTINUOUS   152   *

Joy, Timmy and Izzy and Biker #2 wait as the door is opened.   *

Close on April. When she sees Joy, she gasps. Can't speak.
Then, finally ...

                         APRIL
            Mom --

                                              SCREEN TO WHITE:

153   START MUSIC: *PIECES OF APRIL* BY THREE DOG NIGHT.   153

OVER MUSIC: A series of photographs by Timmy Burns.

The first, April and Joy, during a hug.

Next, the Lee family seated around the table.

A close-up shot of the Waldorf salad.

Interspersed among the Lee family, Izzy and Biker #2, Timmy   *
and Joy now sit.

The green bean casserole.

Izzy carves a piece of turkey for Lee Wai Yam, the mother.   *

Lee Lang, the daughter, Lee Quong, the son, and Timmy, who
holds the camera away from him and takes the picture.

Evette from #19 poses between Joy and April. She holds out a
glass pan filled with cranberry sauce.

A series of three quick photos documenting the arrival of
Jim, Dottie and Beth midway through the meal.

Bobby smiles proudly with his arm around Jim, who forces a
smile.

Dottie makes a face at the camera. Beth seems out of place,
but not wanting to be.

Shots of the turkey carcass.

Joy holding up the Turkey Salt and Pepper Shakers.

A group shot of everyone who shared the meal.

The last photograph is of April and Joy together.

SCENE NOTES

BY PETER HEDGES

Scenes 1 & 2. We never filmed April's dream. Incidentally, the original version of the turkey dream was much bloodier. It concluded with the actual chopping off of a live turkey's head and shots of the turkey running around headless. The scene was a riveting read. But perhaps I had been spending too much time as a novelist, because the logistics and the ethics of chopping off a turkey's head made this scene a questionable proposition.

So I modified it to the version printed on page 1.

But we shot for only sixteen days. Our preliminary schedule left little time for a trip to a turkey farm. It also turned out that the turkeys being grown for that year's Thanksgiving were all tiny little babies. (We were filming in April.) We couldn't find a grown turkey in the tri-state area! So I had to ask myself, "How important is this scene?"

It is most helpful to question the purpose of a scene before one films it. Because if the purpose of the scene is not clear, then it often—in my experience—is a difficult scene to direct. The truth was I found myself defending a scene I couldn't really defend. I suppose I liked it because it seemed a catchy way to start.

Sometimes a simpler, more exquisite solution awaits. Lack of budget and limitations of time, in this case, were a godsend. After three years of writing this script and numerous drafts, a better way became clear. The solution was simple. We'd been looking for ways to show the great love that exists between April and Bobby. Since few things are more intimate than waking up next to someone you love, we turned on the cameras and filmed an hour's worth of footage of Bobby waking up April. Because we'd really had no time to rehearse, this also served as a great way for Katie and Derek to get more comfortable with each other.

Scene 6. April in the script smokes. April in the movie doesn't. We did takes with her smoking, takes with her not smoking. We went with a nonsmoking version because we didn't want to glamorize smoking. Besides there were other, better ways to show April's rebellious side, such as acting.

Scene 7. Mark Livolsi, my astonishing editor, suggested moving this montage later, after Scene 16. He was right.

Scenes 18–32. The order of these scenes has been rearranged. Two significant changes: 1.) The Bobby/April lovemaking/menu scene has been intercut with the Burns family station wagon pulling out of the garage. By cutting back and forth, it creates more energy and a slight comic effect. As in: family heading to visit troubled daughter while daughter is screwing her boyfriend. 2.) We added a scene where April discovers Bobby hanging a decoration outside their door. April: "Bobby, they don't deserve decorations." Bobby: "But you do." They kiss and April pushes Bobby on his way. The scene was added to show how Bobby would rather help April than do anything else.

Scene 33. The clever writer wanted to help the audience understand why during the day Bobby doesn't call in to check on April. As scripted, the scene reveals that Bobby forgot his cell phone. This is just too much work for too little gain. The simpler, better solution was to have April simply lift up her window and scream outside, "Bobby, Bobby!"

Scene 43A. In editing, we deleted Beth's line: "No, we haven't killed her yet." By this point, it's quite clear how Beth feels about April. Also, we deleted Joy's last lines: "Ding Dongs, anyone? Snow Balls. Lil' Debbies . . ." We felt the need for a moment of quiet as the Burns family car drove off.

Scene 47. If you direct a movie, pray that you have someone like Tami Reiker on your side. She was our uncompromising Director of Photography. This scene was not shot in front of a bodega. Tami and I walked around the Lower East Side and she saw potential in a schoolyard where I saw none. The bouncing blue ball was my idea, a visual cue that would help us later in Scene 113, when Bobby meets April's ex-boyfriend. Tami also gets credit for putting Bobby on a motorized scooter as opposed to a silent one and to putting Joy and Timmy on motorcycles rather than in a truck at the end.

Scene 48. The very last few lines of this scene are improvised. Lillias White and Isiah Whitlock, Jr. shot all of their scenes in one day. And it's a tribute to them that they could bring such life and love to those two characters and make us feel as if they'd been married for years.

Scene 50A. On a sixteen-day shoot, you have no time to waste. This traveling car shot was picked up as we drove between locations. The only text change was adding two lines. Timmy: "Uncanny sense of direction." Joy: "Where are we?"

Scene 52. I want to comment about Katie's physical comedy. I encouraged her to make April as violent as possible, whenever possible. In the food preparation scenes, she especially took this to heart, so that when she peels a potato, it's life and death. When she mashes the uncooked potatoes, it's warfare. I'd have her do take after take of these scenes, not because we needed more footage, but because she was so damn funny.

Scene 53. I know nothing about cooking. But my father knows a great deal. He contributed all the various recipe ideas, particularly the Waldorf salad.

Scenes 55-57. The road-kill burial. This sequence had its doubters. Some felt it was too over-the-top. Oliver Platt, who has a keen sense for anything false, felt that Jim digging the hole to bury the poor squirrel was too much. So I shifted that task to the ever-loyal Timmy, played sweetly by John Gallagher, Jr. It's a good example of an actor knowing more than a writer.

Scene 60. The script calls for an old man. We cast our first assistant director, Vebe Borge, who is by no means old. He removed his shirt, so it suggests danger and unwanted intimacy. It's the one of the greatest cameo performances I've ever seen.

Scene 63. This scene illustrates why you want a talented production designer and art director. The script calls for April knocking on a closed door. The film shows a closed door with a portrait of Jesus hanging on the door. April's plea for "Help" takes on new meaning.

Scene 66. We changed Joy's last line: "It's good to have options," and replaced it with Beth's line: "Since when was she [April] in the picture?"

Scene 69. We didn't film Bobby kicking a trashcan. Instead we moved Bobby calling Latrell a second time (Scene 71) into this position.

Scene 70. We deleted Tish's last line: "Now I do have a great recipe for a Meatless Nut Roast." The performance was lovely, but it felt right to stay on April and her dilemma.

Scene 72. This scene was written to play continuously. But the actress playing the Old Woman turned out to be ninety-two years old. Who knew? So we filmed her part of the scene on the first floor. The rest of the scene played on the fourth floor. This was a gift because we also created a new, unscripted scene wherein Bobby makes a call to April and leaves a loving phone message. This was intended to help shore up any doubts about Bobby's loyalties. It also breaks up nicely the crisis April is experiencing.

Scene 76. Remember my cell phone issue from before? What young person doesn't have a cell phone? Well, it may seem a small matter to you, but this issue made me apoplectic. Our solution was to give Latrell a cell phone, have him call from just a few feet away, and see him enter in the reflection of the phone booth.

Scene 77. The Goodwill becomes the Salvation Army because it turns out the Salvation Army had more good will than Goodwill. Also, there are some dialogue trims in Latrell's speech.

Scene 78. I had big plans for this scene, lots of action, but when I went to rehearse it, Oliver Platt gently pulled me aside and said, "Buddy, what are you doing? It's a simple scene. Let it be simple." Mark Livolsi cut it in one pass, and I never changed it. It's one of my favorite scenes.

Scene 79. We ran out of time because the car broke down the same day we shot the Krispy Kreme exterior. Fortunately it was our last day with the car. Fortunately we didn't need Scene 79.

Scenes 81-82. Deleted. Establishing shots of the car moving. It is a source of pride for me that there are no establishing shots in *Pieces of April*.

Scene 83. Our first day of principal photography consisted of shooting all four moving car scenes [Scenes 83, 89, 96, and 99]. For those five actors to film those four scenes on their first day defies comprehension. In this particular scene, Oliver pointed out that Jim had surely heard of black singers, just not Smack Daddy. We came up with a fun exchange wherein he says playfully: "Oh no, I've never heard of James Brown, Barry White . . . Puffy the Dog."

Patty nailed the Smack Daddy speech every time, which I especially appreciated because this speech has particular meaning to me. Let me explain: On what was to be my mother's last birthday, my sister, Mary, suggested I buy Mom a Walkman and a stack of Barry White CDs. It seems she had recently seen Barry White on the *Today* show and she'd entered her "Barry White" phase.

She was bone thin, weak, and in the hospital. But when she put on the new headphones, closed her eyes, and started to move to Barry White's music, it was astonishing. She became like a schoolgirl again—or a young woman listening to jazz in Greenwich Village. She spoke loudly over the music only she could hear: "The thing about Barry is—you know with him it's no one-night stand. Millions want him, but it's as if he's only singing to me, baby."

As she continued, I saw a sexy, wilder side to her I'd never seen before. Her little speech about Barry White was so vivid and spot-on that I asked if she might repeat it. "I'd like to write it down," I told her. "Maybe I'll put it in the script." "You have my permission," she said. "Nothing would make me happier."

We changed Barry White to a fictional singer named Smack Daddy. And I tweaked the text to make it fit better coming from Joy. But it's my mother mostly, and it's the only part of the script that I didn't make up. It's quite likely the best writing I'll ever borrow.

Scene 87. SisQo added some great ad-libs here. "Money green . . . Lapel Surprise." Funny stuff. Wish I'd thought of it.

Scene 88. I wrote an elaborate sequence here where Bobby's new suit is revealed. Too complicated and not enough time. Instead, Bobby simply tries on a suit coat that doesn't fit. Moments later, Latrell brings him a suit he'd been saving for himself, but which he thinks may be more Bobby's size.

Scene 89. This scene I'm particular proud of as it tells us a great deal in a simple way. Timmy is showing his grandmother pictures of his mother. We changed Timmy's line to "These are some photos of Mom I've taken before . . . and now . . ." It's a raw, honest scene, made more so by the anonymous woman who allowed us to use her post-operative mastectomy photograph.

Scene 93. We cut the last two lines of this scene. Bobby's line, "Latrell, that's what love does," is a stronger place to end the scene.

Scenes 94-95. We deleted both shots. One was April back in her apartment, not knowing what to do. At this point in the story, she knows what to do, she just can't always do it. Scene 95 was a shot of the car driving over the hill. If we'd had time to shoot it, we might have used it. But it's not missed.

Scene 97. The stage directions indicate that we should see a *bald* Joy as she goes to put her wig back on. But how many movies have we seen a bald cancer patient? Probably what I'm most proud of in *Pieces of April* is what's *not* said and what you *don't* see. You never Joy's bald head, and you don't see the vomit, and you don't see the violence done to Bobby later on. It allows an audience member to imagine something as opposed to being shown everything.

Scene 99. The "Oh, Mother, don't you just love every day" story is another example of a borrowed moment from my mother and sister's life. I had their blessing. The major difference being my mother remembered who actually said the words.

Joy's kicking the dashboard at the end of the scene was unscripted. It's just another example of allowing an actor to teach you what's possible.

Scene 100–102. This is what I call the *Today* show scene. If Patty or Oliver are ever on the *Today* show it's the scene that Katie Couric would show as a clip. It was a late addition to the script. I knew that to attract great actors I'd need to write great scenes. Joy abandoning the journey and starting to hitchhike back home seemed an ideal way to dramatize her essential struggle. She doesn't want to go visit April, yet she *has* to go visit April. I'd also been looking for a way to give Joy and Jim a scene alone. Lastly, here was a chance for quiet and loyal Jim to stand up and take charge of the situation.

Scenes 111–112. We simplified the action of these scenes with the Chinese family. Time was a factor, but it had more to do with the momentum of the story and not wanting to slow it down.

Scene 113. This scene was split into two parts. Bobby exits the bodega with flowers. We changed the Older Woman's line from, "Don't you look good," to "Tyrone's looking for you." In the second half of the scene, we see Bobby scooter through the schoolyard, only to be stopped by the same bouncing blue ball from before. The idea was to return to something familiar and be surprised by who we then meet. The other important change to the scene was the choice to ignore the final stage direction: *Then Bobby runs.* This allowed us to delete the Bobby being chased sequence (Scenes 114, 116, 118, and 120) which was a huge time-saver. But more importantly, I had never been happy with the idea of the chase. It always felt false, as if the writer was trying to generate some kind of suspense. Besides, Derek Luke's Bobby wouldn't run. He's surrounded by a group of young thugs, so what does he do? He drops his shoulder bag, faces his situation straight on, and says: "Let's go." If he has to fight, he will.

Scene 121. Oliver and I talked a great deal about this scene where Jim thinks Joy might have died. The first scripted versions were much more "dramatic" in that Jim pulled the car over suddenly and panicked. But what we ultimately came up with is much better. It's a quiet moment and we stay on Jim as he notices something, then grows concerned, pulls over. Then, and only then, do we realize why he's stopping. He reaches out, touches Joy, she moves slightly, still alive. His hands cover his face. In the script, Joy is supposed to wake up and see Jim crying. We decided to let Joy sleep and let Jim have this moment to himself, mostly. I added two lines which come from the back seat. Dottie: "Why did we stop?" Beth: "Daddy thought . . ."

Scenes 130–131. We decided to break up scene 131. We play the first part of the scene where the family sees April's building for the first time. They're all horrified. Jim says under his breath, "Goddammit, April." Then we cut to Scene 130 where the repaired turkey is revealed by the Chinese Family. Then we cut to Beth screaming. Bobby arrives, all bloody, saying, "Welcome, welcome." This was the first scene that Derek filmed. It's an extremely delicate moment. Minutes later the family will be driving off. And why? Because Bobby is black? Because they're scared? Racist? I didn't want it to feel like they were fleeing because of race. So we did many takes of this scene because I wanted options when we edited. Derek did angry versions and sweet versions and every other kind of version in between. Another reason for the numerous takes was that I started to pare away the text. I'd written lines wherein Bobby professed his love for April. "I'm Bobby. The Bobby who loves your daughter. The Bobby who would do anything for her." These lines were not necessary. They are a great example of a writer not trusting his story. It's much better to see how Bobby loves April earlier in the film than to hear him explain it later. Here's an obvious thought: Film is a visual medium. When we started to shoot, and Derek was "bloodied up" for the scene, it became exceedingly clear why the Burns family would flee, and why not a lot of words were needed. We'd watched Bobby spend a big part of the movie trying to get an outfit to look nice when he meets her family. They show up, his clothes are torn, his lip is bloody. What's terrific in Derek's performance is the purity of heart and the lack of self-pity.

Scene 132–133. These scenes were combined to play inside April's apartment. We added some lines for April to be more concerned about Bobby's physical condition and for Bobby to be more concerned about April's family. She doesn't put on a Band-Aid, as scripted, but she starts for the bathroom. Bobby stops her and tells her that her family is downstairs. "They're downstairs waiting for you. Go. Go!"

Scene 136. We cut all the dialogue and changed the scene so that it was a simple exterior shot of the Burns family car as it drives away. The scene needed to answer only one essential question: Where did the family go?

Scene 140. This is the scene where April cracks open. As scripted, Bobby was to comfort her, hug her, but when we went to film it, it felt wrong. I love these performances. Katie is heartbreaking. Derek, as Bobby, sits nearby watching, waiting with love for her great grief to pass. We cut April's line, "I knew it, I just knew it." It felt far better for April to say only one line in between sobs: "What are we gonna do with all the food?"

Scene 141. Deleted. No establishing shots.

Scene 142. We changed Beth's line from "You did the right thing" to "*We* did the right thing."

Also, we never shot the angle on Joy as she's looking back at them. I was worried we'd never believe she'd get on the motorcycle and go back to April. So I built in all sorts of tiny moments that I hoped would accumulate. But it became clear as we edited that we didn't need many of these moments.

Scene 143. This is a critical scene. It's the moment where Joy comes to her senses. It's a scene that always read well, but when we went to shoot it, it played like something from a bad soap opera. We weren't helped by the fact that we had an hour to shoot the scene. The bathroom was tiny, too, so the camera could be placed in only one position. But something was very wrong and I couldn't figure it out. In a moment of near panic, I turned to Dianne Dreyer (Script Supervisor/Associate Producer) and Tami Reiker (Director of Photography), and I said, "I'm stumped. Help." They talked me through the scene. Dianne suggested that this is a moment of great vulnerability. The young actress playing the Young Girl happened to be a friend's daughter. She was wearing tights. Dianne suggested that she might be caught with her tights down and that Joy would watch in the mirror as the girl pulled up her tights. This physical action would trigger something in Joy, remind her of a younger April. It was done in one take and it worked well, I thought. But because we couldn't get a close-up of Patty as she looked at the girl, we decided to re-shoot the scene. (It's the only scene we did re-shoot.) In our second try, we were able to replicate all the terrific aspects of the first attempt but also get close on Joy, see all the subtle shifts that occur in Patty's face. Re-cutting this scene with Mark Livolsi was like Christmas in July. (We were cutting in July.) Patty's performance was so human and complex.

Scene 144. We changed Joy's line to the Motorcycle Guy from "Is one of those yours?" to a simpler, less leading, "Excuse me?"

Scene 146. We deleted Joy's line, "What's your name?" In fact Joy never speaks again in the movie. Her actions do the speaking.

Scene 148. We deleted Jim's lines as well. It's more powerful for him to be silent. Only Beth is nattering on. Jim can't bring himself to speak.

Scene 150. I knew when we shot this scene that we'd probably cut it. For Joy to be flirting with the Motorcycle Man or spending energy on anything other than getting to April as quickly as possible was a mistake. It's the only scene in the movie that we shot that didn't make it into the finished film.

Scene 152. We shot Katie's last moment on her first day. It had to do with schedule and locations. It was not an ideal way to shoot the scene. But she was terrific. We did a series of takes where she said, "Mom." And a few where she didn't. We went with her silence. It was all in her face.

Scene 153. Tami Reiker had the idea to shoot the end in two different ways. Sam Levy, who operated our second camera, took still photographs with the Sony PD-150 video camera. Tami shot actual footage. I didn't understand why until she explained that it would be good to have options. I'm really grateful she did because it made the final montage a much more compelling sequence. We cut many versions of the ending. The one constant was the lovely moment between Beth and April when they hug and Beth tries not to cry. The script suggests that the last shot be of April and Joy, but this felt too easy and obvious. Also, at some point we settled on the reprise of the camera timer—and it's incessant tick—and the final click leading us to a black screen. Gary Winick pushed for a more economical sequence and he was right. Originally we used the Three Dog Night song, as scripted, but at the persistent, gentle urging of John Lyons, I met with several composers, the last being one of my favorite musicians in all the world, Stephin Merritt. We showed him the film and he liked it except for the "Pieces of April" song. He felt it was too sentimental, sappy. So he wrote something for us, which he played on his ukulele. The song is perfect.

One final note: More often than not, as we tried to set up *Pieces of April*, studio executives and money people would argue that the ending was insufficient. "We need to have a scene between April and Joy. We need to hear them reconcile, or whatever." We knew this was not the case. The whole journey of this movie is not toward some exchange of words. The story is about a girl trying to cook a turkey for her dying mother and a dying mother who'd rather be anywhere else than with her estranged daughter. It's not about what they say to each other. It's about getting to a place where they can speak to each other. That they're in each other's presence—and for one moment, there is grace—that's all that matters. Then we cut to black—because even moments of grace can't last forever.

ADDENDUM: THE ORIGINAL OPENING

In November 1999, I had an informal reading of eighty tentative pages for a script I'd entitled *Pieces of April*. A few friends and I read the pages and while the problems were numerous, there was a story at the core. This reading was rather instructive. For instance, the character of Joy was different from the role I ultimately wrote. In that first attempt, she was sweet and wise and cloying. Dottie, on the other hand, had all the venom and all the fun. It became clear this was a mistake. Not only was Joy dying, but I'd made her a saint. If ever there was a time to make a character unsympathetic, this was it. Joy should be anything but joyful. She is running out of time, so she should be pissed and incendiary and painfully honest.

Below you will find the very first opening for *Pieces of April*. These twelve pages dealt with how April learned about her mother's condition and how April and Bobby met. They were by far my favorite pages from that day. It was a blow when one of my good, smart friends suggested that I cut all twelve pages. But it was a good suggestion. It's much better—and more difficult—to start the movie on Thanksgiving Day. I'm including the very first opening not only because I like the pages, but because they evidence an important screenwriting truth: Just because you don't film certain scenes doesn't mean you shouldn't have written them.

EXT. LOWER EAST SIDE - NYC - EVENING

A car turns onto the street on the Lower East Side, near
Tompkins Square Park, in Alphabet City.

A MAN, middle aged, drives slowly, glancing at both sides of
the street.

POV from inside car: A run-down bodega on the corner; an
abandoned building nearby; a vacant lot with a garden of
rusted sculptures, with a sign which reads NO TRESPASSING.

LOUD MUSIC (sung in Spanish) blares from a passing ghetto
blaster.

Other side of the street: A HOMELESS MAN sleeps on the
street with a torn garbage bag of belongings nearby.

The car slows down and stops in front of a shop with its grey
metal security door still down.

In front of the gate, FIVE TEENAGE SLACKERS, four boys, one
girl, sit leaning against the gate. They're dressed in black
boots and black, torn clothes. With a wild array of
hairstyles (shaved heads, Mohawks, colorful dye jobs),
multiple tattoos and pierced body parts, they sit motionless
and stare out coldly. A mutt dog sits on a ragged leash next
to them.

The Man in the car looks at a small photo he's holding. He
looks up at the Five Teenagers. The GIRL, stares at him for
a moment, exhales from her cigarette and looks away.

The Man pushes open the car door and climbs out of the car.

He approaches the Five Teenagers.

                    MAN
          April?

The dog GROWLS. The Girl glares at him, with angry, almost
dead eyes.

                    MAN (cont'd)
          Are you April?

He extends the photograph.

The photo is of a clean-cut girl with a pink sweater and a
slight perm in her hair.

The Girl laughs.

                                                (CONTINUED)

CONTINUED:

                    MAN (cont'd)
          Maybe one of you knows her.

The Dog barks and the Man hurries out of reach of its teeth.

LATER:

The Man approaches a Middle Aged Hispanic Woman walking with
a sack of groceries.

                    MAN
               (extending the picture)
          Excuse me?

                    WOMAN
          No habla engles.

                    MAN
          If you could just look at ...

The Woman hurries on.

LATER:

An OLD MAN looks at the picture. He grunts in recognition
and points to ...

A run down, white brick tenement building in the middle of
the block.

EXT. WHITE BRICK TENEMENT BUILDING

The Man looks through the dirty door window, trying to look
into the building where April may be staying. He pulls at
the front door, but it's locked.

EVEN LATER:

Wearied, the Man takes out a cigarette, puts it in his mouth.
He feels his pockets for matches. No luck. He glances
toward the Five Teenagers. They haven't moved.

The Man grows almost frantic in his matches search, checking
the same places two, three times.

                    GIRL (O.S.)
          Here.

The Man turns, a GIRL in her early twenties, bleached hair, a
pierced navel, a tattoo of a rose on her shoulder, strikes a
match.

                                                  (CONTINUED)

CONTINUED:

                    MAN
          Thank you ... April.

April looks at him, surprised he knows her name.

The Man produces a business card. As April reads it:

                    MAN (cont'd)
          You need to call home.

EXT. PHONE BOOTH AT END OF THE STREET - MINUTES LATER

April is at a pay phone. The Man stands at a respectful
distance.

                    APRIL
               (faintly, into the receiver)
          It's me.

The Man smiles, his job done.

While April talks, the Man turns away and sees ...

Man's POV: Down the street, a metal trash can stands,
overturned, on the roof of his car. The car has been covered
in trash.

The Man hurries down the street toward his car. He glares at
the Five Teenagers ...

The Five Teenagers, still sitting there, continue their cold,
blank stares, as if the Man does not exist. The Man begins
to pick the trash off his car, when he glances back at April
and sees ...

Man's POV (LONG SHOT): The phone booth empty, the receiver
dangling.

MEDIUM SHOT: The phone booth empty, the receiver dangling.

CLOSE UP: The receiver dangling, swinging still, from having
just been dropped.

INT. TENEMENT APARTMENT BUILDING - STAIRWELL

Fighting back tears, April climbs the steps of her run down
building.

She passes a NEIGHBOR who is locking her door. The Neighbor
sighs disapprovingly as April passes.

WE HEAR the sound of April's keys jangling...

INT. APARTMENT HALLWAY - OUTSIDE DOOR TO APARTMENT #13

On her door, an "Eviction Notice" has been posted.

April rips it off.

She unlocks her door, goes inside, the door slams.

                                                    CUT TO:

INT. SUPPORT GROUP - ST. MARK'S PLACE

Close on April who sits among a large group of people, all
ages and races, their chairs arranged in an irregular circle.

                    GROUP MEMBER (O.S.)
          And I feel good to have, you know, *done
          something* ...

                    TIME KEEPER (O.S.)
          Time.

                    GROUP MEMBER (O.S.)
          So OK, that's it. Keep coming back. It
          works if you work it.

April meekly raises her hand as others raise their hands more
enthusiastically.

The Group Leader points to April.

                         APRIL
               (trying to smile)
          Hi, I'm April. And I'm ... a mess.

                    THE GROUP
               (almost in unison)
          Hi April.

Beat.

                    APRIL
          It's my mom.

April drops her head and sobs.

Shots of the others watching - some supportive, sympathetic,
some annoyed, impatient. The sound of April crying
continues.

                                              DISSOLVE TO:

                                              (CONTINUED)

CONTINUED:

The Time Keeper staring at his watch.

                    TIME KEEPER
          Time.

Other group members raise their hands. The Group Leader
points at someone who we do not see yet.

                    MAN (O.S.)
          Hi. I'm Bobby. I'm an addict-drunk-
          debtor-over eater ... I'm so many things--

Someone laughs.

                    BOBBY (O.S.)
          And I'm not trying to be funny.
                    (Beat)
          Sometimes it gets to me. You know, all
          the talking, everybody talking, the whole
          world talking and talking, and sometimes
          it's just too much. But then, what you
          said ... *you* ...

April looks up and sees ...

Bobby, a striking young black man with a scar on his left
cheek.

                    BOBBY (cont'd)
          I'm sorry, I forgot your name.

April looks away.

                    BOBBY (cont'd)
          But I'll never forget what you said. Or
          what you didn't say. It was real. And
          we all felt it. And even though I don't
          know you, I know you. I'm not you, but
          I'm like you. See, moms, we all have
          moms ... and let me say, *if* your mother
          loves you, *no one loves you like your
          mom.*

At this moment Bobby is starting to hate the sound of his own
voice. He tries to quickly finish his share.

                    BOBBY (cont'd)
          What am I saying? I don't know what I'm
          saying. What am I saying?
          I'd like to thank you for what you said.
          I mean, for how you said what you didn't
          say.

CONTINUED: (2)

Bobby looks at ...

April who is looking right back at him.

                                        CUT TO:

INT. APRIL'S APARTMENT - LATER THAT NIGHT

In dim light, April and Bobby are fucking. As if the world
were about to end.

                                        CUT TO:

INT. APRIL'S APARTMENT - MORNING

Sunlight streams through a white lace curtain.

                    APRIL (O.S.)
          I can't. Not right now.

April and Bobby lie on a mattress on the floor.

                    APRIL
          But thanks for asking. I just can't talk
          about her. Okay?

Bobby starts to gently stroke her hair.

                    APRIL
          You're sweet, I think.

Bobby smiles.

                    APRIL
          We could talk about something else, if
          you want. We could talk about mistakes.
          As in: Did we just make one? I've made
          so many. I try to think of mine as a
          kind of preparation for something ... I
          don't know ... better? Maybe the mistake
          is to think it was a mistake. Maybe I've
          never been so right before, never been so
          wise, maybe we just knew, and it was
          right, and we knew it, because of our
          mistakes, and good for us, for knowing--

Bobby wipes the tears from April's eyes. Beat.

                    APRIL
          I, I just couldn't take it if what we did
          was ...
               (mouthing the following)
          ... a *mistake*.

                                        (CONTINUED)

CONTINUED:

Beat. Bobby sees something.

> BOBBY
> Is that clock right?

> APRIL
> It doesn't work.

Bobby sits up, reaches for his pants. He checks the watch in his pocket.

> BOBBY
> Crap.

INT. HALLWAY OUTSIDE APRIL'S APARTMENT - MOMENTS LATER

Bobby, trying to finish dressing as he leaves, comes out the door. April watches.

> BOBBY
> Look, it's not you ...

> APRIL
> OK, go.

> BOBBY
> I'm sorry --

> APRIL
> Go!

> BOBBY
> I'll explain later.

> APRIL
> Goodbye!

April slams the door. Beat. She lets her head drop against the door.

> APRIL
> (to herself)
> I'm an asshole.

                                            CUT TO:

INT. PROBATION OFFICE - DAY

A wall clock reads 10:10.

At a table, Bobby speaks with Mac, a burly man.

                                        (CONTINUED)

CONTINUED:

                    MAC
              (over it)
         Bobby, Bobby, Bobby.

                    BOBBY
         I said I'm sor(ry)--

                    MAC
         You don't get it.

                    BOBBY
         I do, I do.

                    MAC
         No, you don't. So I'm forced to be
         exceedingly clear. *Are you listening,
         Bobby!*

                    BOBBY

         Yes, sir.

                    MAC
         I hope so. Because I'm the best friend
         you got here, and I don't even like you.

                    BOBBY
         OK!

                    MAC
         Do not raise your voice. That's the
         thing, the anger thing, you *say* you've
         changed. And then you ...

                    BOBBY
         OK.

                    MAC
         If you so much as hop a turnstile, if you
         jaywalk the slightest little bit, if you
         are unkind to some old lady ... are you
         liste--

                    BOBBY
         I'm listeni--

                    MAC
         You better be, buddy, because if you're
         even a second late to your next
         appointment with me, you'll be hauled off
         to Rikers.
              (pause, for effect)
         And Bobby?

                                        (CONTINUED)

CONTINUED: (2)

                    BOBBY
          Yes.

                    MAC
          You don't want to go to Rikers. And do
          you know why?

                    BOBBY
          Well ...

                    MAC
          You're kind of cute, Bobby.

                    BOBBY
          Thanks.

                    MAC
          Don't get smart with me. There are a lot
          of guys in Rikers who would like nothing
          more than to fuck you in the ass. You
          wouldn't last a day. They'd split you in
          two. Am I clear?

                    BOBBY
          Very.

                    MAC
          Good.
               (suddenly, creepily pleasant)
          So, how you been?

                                                  CUT TO:

INT. PORT AUTHORITY BUS STATION

A Greyhound bus parked at Terminal 18. It's about to depart.
The destination sign reads ALLENTOWN.

                    BUS DRIVER
          Last call for Allentown.

April sits on a bench with a small bag. She holds a ticket.

                    BUS DRIVER
          Miss, are you coming?

April appears terrified, stares back motionless for a moment.
Then, almost imperceptibly, she shakes her head "no."

The bus driver disappears into the bus.

                                                  (CONTINUED)

CONTINUED:

Close on April as the sound of the door WHOOSHES closed, and
the engine RARES UP.

                                              CUT TO:

INT. DOJOS - ST. MARK'S PLACE

April takes the last bite of a vegetarian burger. She's been
talking with a FRIEND, who is also her waitress.

                    WAITRESS FRIEND
                (tearing the check off her pad)
            Look, I'd have gotten on the bus, but
            that's just me--

                    APRIL
            You think you're helping--

                    WAITRESS FRIEND
            All I'm saying is we're just different--

                    APRIL
            But you're not helping.

                    WAITRESS FRIEND
            What I mean is: My parents (mom) didn't
            kick me out.

Beat. (Ouch.)

                    WAITRESS FRIEND (cont'd)
            Maybe you're just not ready.

                    APRIL
            It's not like there's an endless amount
            of time.

                    WAITRESS FRIEND
            There never is. And your problem isn't
            that you're too selfish. If anything,
            you're too generous.

                    APRIL
                (suddenly cracking)
            I don't know what to do. And nobody can
            tell me.

                    WAITRESS FRIEND
                (noticing something out the
                 window)
            Who's that?

April looks out window.

                                              (CONTINUED)

CONTINUED:

Bobby stands there, gives an apologetic half wave.

                                              CUT TO:

EXT. SECOND AVENUE - NIGHT

April walks fast down Second Avenue, pursued by Bobby.

                    APRIL
          Leave me alone!

                    BOBBY
          I knew it, I knew it.

                    APRIL
          Back off!

                    BOBBY
          You gotta let me explain ...

April suddenly turns to him, but continues walking backwards.

                    APRIL
          Listen, you little fucker. Not one of
          these tears is for you. OK? Do you
          understand? *You are nowhere in these
          tears!*
               (turning back around)
          And that's probably hard for you to
          believe!

                    BOBBY
          Please give me a chance to explain!

                    APRIL
          You're selfish. WHY DO I KNOW THAT? WHY
          DO YOU THINK I KNOW THAT?!!! BECAUSE ...
               (Quoting and mocking)
          "Even though I don't know you, I know
          you. I'm not you, but I'm like you."

The initial chirp and ensuing cry of a nearby police car.
Police lights FLASH as a car approaches.

                    APRIL (cont'd)
          Selfish, and terrible, thinking only
          about myself ...

April has stopped walking and moves back and forth.

Only now does Bobby notice the Police Car as it stops
suddenly.

                                            (CONTINUED)

CONTINUED:

                    BOBBY
           (turning to the police as they
           climb out of their cars)
      What? What did I do? We're talking. It
      is not against the law to talk!

As the police try to question Bobby, he keeps talking over
the police inquiries.

Close on April, who turns around ...

                    BOBBY (O.S.) (cont'd)
      She's my friend. I'm -- please --
      I'm a good person -- I'd just like her to
      see that!

                    POLICE OFFICER (O.S.)
      Stop shouting.

                    BOBBY (O.S.)
      You'd be shouting. I don't want --

April looks in the window and sees ...

Amidst antiques stacked throughout the room, and in the
middle of the room, a beautiful oak table with place settings
has been set out, as if for a Thanksgiving meal.

                    BOBBY (O.S.) (cont'd)
      To miss -- my chance. This may be my
      only chance!

April freezes as she's something that captures her eye ...

Close on two ceramic turkey salt and pepper shakers.

                    POLICEMAN (O.S.)
      Ma'am, are you all right?

April, still staring at the salt and pepper shakers, smiles.

                                        SCREEN TO WHITE:

STILLS

The last day of shooting for the Burns family. The first day of shooting for April and
Bobby. (From left to right: Producer John Lyons, Derek Luke, Alice Drummond,
Oliver Platt, Writer/Director Peter Hedges, Katie Holmes, Patricia Clarkson, John
Gallagher, Jr., and Alison Pill)

Katie Holmes stars as April Burns, a young woman who can't get her turkey cooked.

Derek Luke as Bobby, April's devoted boyfriend.

Bobby and his friend Latrell (SisQo) outside of the Salvation Army.

Jim (Oliver Platt) escorts Dottie (Alice Drummond) to the Burns family car. Beth (Alison Pill) reintroduces herself: "Hi, Grandma. I'm Beth, your *granddaughter*."

Writer/Director Peter Hedges discusses the scene with Oliver Platt and Alice Drummond.

Patricia Clarkson between takes.

Oliver Platt as Jim Burns, listening to his son Timmy say: "It was a squirrel, I think. Or a small raccoon."

Patricia Clarkson as Joy Burns.

The road-kill burial. Beth, Jim, and Joy listen as Timmy says: "We're sorry we didn't know
you. We hope it was quick. . . ."

Alison Pill as Beth Burns.

John Gallagher, Jr., as Timmy Burns.

Katie Holmes and Sean Hayes between takes.

Sean Hayes as Wayne with the new stove.

April comes downstairs to greet her family, but they're gone.

Patricia Clarkson and Peter Hedges discuss the next shot.

Joy climbs on a motorcycle that will take her to April.

April serves the Chinese family a Thanksgiving meal.

Peter Hedges, happy.

AFTERWORD

TALKING WITH PETER HEDGES
BY ROB FELD

When he was an eighth-grader in Iowa, Peter Hedges read Stanislavski's *Building a Character* and *An Actor Prepares*, determined to spend his life as an actor. He did theater in high school, studied ballet, modern dance, and voice, and went to Interlochen theater camp for the summer. At 18, he followed this path to the North Carolina School of the Arts but eventually found, he will tell you, "the harder I worked, the better everyone else got!"

He was too young, he didn't know himself well enough, or he simply wasn't meant to be an actor, but it occurred to Hedges that he had classmates who were struggling, too. He thought that he could write something for them that would show just how terrifically talented they were. When his fellow students saw Hedges' first play, *Oregon*, which was mounted in the school's lighting lab, the response was overwhelmingly enthusiastic. Having no idea that it would trigger that kind of response, he thought, "Here I am trying to be an actor all these years, and I've never done anything that has affected people as much as this play that I wrote. Every egg from every basket had been put into this idea of being an actor, but maybe playwriting is the direction I'm supposed to go in."

Doing just that, Hedges graduated and moved to New York in 1984, starting a theater company with Mary-Louise Parker and Joe Mantello, among others. For three years, Hedges wrote and directed all the company's plays, mounting them in obscure, illegal spaces. He modeled his company after Steppenwolf, which demonstrated to Hedges "what can happen when you work with people who believe in each other." Nevertheless, years of New York temp jobs followed, during which time Hedges hardly lived anywhere for more than a few months at a time. Wherever rent was free or cheap, he would land, trying to write as much as possible. While he was workshopping a play at Circle Rep, Hedges started another play for his company called *Other Grapes*. Finding that it wasn't working as a play, Hedges transformed it into the novel that would become *What's Eating Gilbert Grape*.

Then came one of those bizarre twists of fate that make careers. Lasse Hallström's film teacher, Ingvar Skogsberg, who had become a translator of novels from English to Swedish, read *Gilbert Grape*. He called Hallström and said, "Either you or Milos Forman needs to make a movie of this book."

"The next thing I know," says Hedges, "I'm having lunch with Lasse Hallström." He must not have spilled any soup on his tie because Hallström offered to let this first-timer not just write the script, but hang around the set and learn as well.

This was an enormous learning opportunity for Hedges, who, until this point, had written plays and prose, but never a screenplay. Under Hallström's tutelage, Hedges learned the power of the cut, the differences in an audience's suspension of disbelief between theater and film, and the skill of visual storytelling. Scene by scene, he learned to encapsulate a moment within a handful of words, eliminating pages of dialogue that would have worked on stage, but been death on screen. The resulting adaptation was an atmospheric film, both brooding and full of love, which maintained Hedges' voice and humor, and established him as a writer of depth and versatility.

While Hedges' Oscar nomination this year for *About a Boy* was thrilling, it is easy to see how close to his heart is his new film, *Pieces of April*, which he directed and shot low-budget on digital video. As a result of the collaborative, common-goal process, Hedges described *Pieces of April* as "probably the purest experience I may ever get to have in the movie business," and it shows. When the film premiered at Sundance 2003, its impending sale to a distributor immediately became the popular topic of festival scuttlebutt. Though rumors of bidding wars and cloak-and-dagger salesmanship ran rampant, Hedges described the process as very up-front and pleasant, and before the festival was through it was announced that *Pieces of April* had been bought by United Artists for theatrical distribution.

Pieces of April was the first screenplay Hedges would attempt to make that was not an adaptation of a book, as even *Gilbert Grape* had been, albeit his own. It was also the first he would attempt to direct. This may have been due to the intensely personal reasons that led Hedges to write it. Though an entirely fictional story, the film was impacted by Hedges' experience of his mother dying from cancer, and how he and his family coped.

Pieces of April is about a misfit Lower East Side girl named April (Katie Holmes) who tries to cook a Thanksgiving dinner for her family, who is traveling to New York for the occasion. Despite what could have been heavy subject matter, the film functions excellently as a comedy. Within the context of such extreme circumstances, Clarkson's skillful handling of Hedges' wry wit helps the film focus on the persistence and absurdity of life's banal moments, rather than getting bogged down in the heavy, melodramatic scenes of illness. Though an impending death serves as the plot's motor, the same sense of mortality that marked *What's Eating Gilbert Grape* provides for much of the film's deep humor. It is his success with this balancing act that has helped set Hedges apart. He can create a world of beautifully resonant subject matter which slips in under a cynical modern audience's radar while it's laughing. As a writer, Hedges gets The Great Joke but consistently meets it with a signature combination of irony and humanist warmth that allows you to leave the theater with both a smile and a sense of understanding, because what he has served up for you is palatable truth.

Rob: Coming from theater, with Gilbert Grape as your first screenplay, it must have been an incredible learning experience under Lasse.

Peter: When I met with Lasse, he said, "Well, what do you want to do?" I said that my real dream was to write and direct films, but, you know, I didn't anticipate that he would ask me to write the screenplay. I knew that novelists often didn't get to adapt their own work, but, based upon reading the book and meeting me, he said "I think you should try writing the script, and I'll also let you be involved in casting, location scouting, editing, the whole process, that way you'll learn a great deal." That was his promise and he kept it.

Rob: That's amazing.

Peter: It wasn't always easy. If you've never written a screenplay and suddenly the first script you've written is being made, and you're in pre-production before the script's done, and you have parts of the script you can't make work because you're trying to distill your own novel, which you still don't maybe understand . . . well, I felt overwhelmed and, at times, in way over my head. The big difficulty of taking *Gilbert Grape* and making it a movie was that the novel was written in an unreliable first-person narrative. The character is very bitter—wonderfully bitter and reductive in how he describes people in his life. Lasse would constantly make the case that we cannot shoot the movie in the tone that the book is written because we will be making fun of the people. He has a very acute sense of, and an aversion to, reductive writing and the simplification and shrinking of people. Ironically, the book ends with Gilbert moving from a two-dimensional view of the people in his life to a much more complete view of them. So, there was a tone issue, but also an issue that I came from the theater and tried to achieve everything through dialogue. I didn't know what I was doing. It was a great education. What I found when we did *Pieces of April* was that I referenced those *Gilbert Grape* experiences because I wanted to make a movie that was intensely human. It needed to feel real, authentic. These characters must feel like people and not caricatures. Adrienne Rich, one of my favorite poets, wrote that a lie is a shortcut through another person. So, if I take a shortcut through a character in my writing, then I'm lying, and I didn't want to lie.

When I look back at the *Gilbert Grape* experience, I have to laugh at myself. I remember one instance where it was going to rain in a scene. I was very concerned about the believability of the rain. Three scenes before the rain scene I wrote in the stage directions: It's overcast. Two scenes before: Rumble of thunder in the distance. One scene before: Light drops of rain begin to fall. When I arrived on set, I saw that it was a bright sunny day and it was the scene where light drops of rain were supposed to fall. I was beside myself. When Lasse asked what was wrong, I told him. He explained that in a movie when we cut to a scene with rain the audience figures out its raining. You see, I was very concerned with a kind of logic that wasn't necessarily a cinematic logic.

My favorite scene in the movie is one of the last I wrote. It's the scene where Gilbert's lover, Mrs. Betty Carver (Mary Steenburgen) comes to say goodbye to Gilbert (Johnny Depp) after her husband has died. All through the movie he's been developing this relationship with Becky (Juliette Lewis). It needed to be acknowledged that there had been this other relationship, but I could never figure out how. I wrote so many versions of this scene—some of them were 5-6 pages long. My final version of the scene was the simplest. As Mrs. Carver exits the grocery store, she turns to Becky and says, "He's all yours." After she's gone, Becky asks Gilbert, "You gonna miss her?" "Yes," Gilbert says. Then Becky looks away and says, "Good." Nine words.

Rob: *In general, economy is an amazing lesson to learn.*

Peter: Yes. Now what I'm most proud of in *Pieces of April* is what's *not* said and what you *don't* see. You never see the mother's bald head, and you don't see the vomit, and you don't see the violence. It allows an audience member to be a participant in the telling of the story, as opposed to being told everything. If I aspire to anything it's to tell stories that are easy to understand but are hard to handle. With Lasse, there isn't an arch, postmodern irony to his world view. He has a big-hearted view of people. From working with him, I think I'm more able now to be sincere. Nothing sentimental or sappy, but to be direct; to say, This is what this story is, this is who these people are, and this is what happens on this day, when these people collide.

Rob: *Knowing that you would direct* Pieces of April, *did that affect how you wrote it?*

Peter: I wasn't conscious of writing it differently than I would write a script for someone else. I tend to write pretty leanly. I don't over-describe. There's not much description in my screenplays anyway. There were definitely times when I started to write a scene and I would say, "Wait, wait, wait. I would have to direct this! So, maybe it could be simpler . . ." I also assumed that we wouldn't have much money, so I was thinking budgetarily, too. But I found those limitations liberating. I think if I were given a ridiculous sum of money and told that there were no limits, I would have a harder time writing than I do when I know I have these actors and this much money and this many days. It may be borne out of my early theater experiences, where we just learned to make do with little. I think the great part of that exercise is to find out what's essential.

Rob: *Limitations are actually questions being asked of you, which can be good to play off of.*

Peter: Yes, limitations ask questions. So, if you say, No, I *have* to have an elephant, then there better be a pretty good reason for the elephant.

I've found that it's best for me to write every script in such a way that I'd want to direct it. Write it so that I'm desperate to direct it but assume that I probably won't be asked. This way I still have to make sure that it's clear, that it's vivid, that it can be followed. You know, it's curious that I'm a novelist and I resist writing detailed description, which is often the bread and butter of being a novelist. Maybe I'm not a novelist, I just pose as one.

Rob: How did you find music functioning as you were writing, and changing your script as you put it in?

Peter: Very interesting question. I do find, as a general rule, most American films are over-scored. The music is used to evoke emotion, when it would be better if it was the story doing the work.

Rob: What is bad dialogue to you, as you read it?

Peter: Bad dialogue tells you something that you could have figured out on your own. I would say that good screenwriting dialogue is essential dialogue. Mind you, I did watch *Pulp Fiction* the other night. There's just something delicious about the language, but it's often a misdirect. Something else is going on. He lulls you into this riff, and it's great language, but then something happens. He gets you giggling, gets you thinking about something else, then—Bam!—the gun goes off. But, if he was conveying key plot information with all of that dialogue, it would be much less interesting. You know, as a playwright, you lead with dialogue, so it's been a real process of finding that balance. Understanding what makes a movie different from a play. You can be a great dialogue writer, but it doesn't make you a great screenwriter.

Rob: Let's talk about adaptation vs. doing an original work. You adapted your own novel, the novels **A Map of the World** *and* **About a Boy, Pieces of April** *is original, and now you're adapting* **The Devil Wears Prada.**

Peter: Of the eight screenplays that I've written, seven have been adaptations. I can't even count the number of original screenplays I've attempted. I think a great way to learn how to write a screenplay is to adapt someone else's work. They do say that a novel is closer to a screenplay than a play is—for what it's worth. An original screenplay was the harder thing for me to do.

When I adapt someone else's book, I look for those one or two moments in a story that I've never seen before—and those are the reasons for the movie. I build everything around those one or two moments. I found in writing *Gilbert Grape* that I had to let so much go. That was probably the best training for screenwriting. Learning what to let go.

Rob: *What are the characters that attract you, even if they're adapted?*

Peter: Well, my primary vocation is as a novelist, so most of the characters that I've written in my life have been original. They tend to be people who are complicated. I like people who are messy, who surprise me when I write them. People who I don't necessarily approve of but, having known them, feel compassion for. From the obese mother in *Gilbert Grape*—who has total love for her family, but such total hate for herself that she would let herself get to the state that she's in—to Joy—who is dying in *Pieces of April*, who is so angry, and ultimately does the right thing—to, if you know my plays, some really wild characters. A lot of my stronger characters tend to be women, which I'm particularly proud of. You know, I started writing because I love actors and because I trained as one, and I know what actors love to do. They love to be surprising and to go a lot of places. So I strive to write parts that I think really good actors would want to play. One of my favorite actresses was Geraldine Page, and what I loved about her was that she could spin on a dime. She could be laughing, turn away, and she'd turn back and tears would be running down her face. It's that capacity to inhabit the ridiculous and the sublime. The common and the extraordinary. The ugly and the beautiful. Those dichotomies dropped right next to each other. That's when it's fun.

Rob: *In 2000 I talked to Alex Payne and Jim Taylor, and then just a few weeks ago talked to them again. After* Election, *I asked them if it was harder to tell a straight, intimate story like* Ordinary People, *these days. Do audiences trust it less? Jim, in particular, talked about how aware he was of being part of that ironic humor-thing, and would like, in a sense, to move beyond that.*

So, when they made **About Schmidt** ***I read their comments back to them, because they had moved beyond, but had maintained, their unmistakable voice.***

Peter: I think your assessment of their progression is really accurate. For me, it may also be a response to 9/11. After that happened—it was just right across the river from my office, here—I looked at everything that I was working on—a new novel, notes for plays—and I asked myself, "In view of the overt fragility that is now our world, what really matters?" There was a paralysis in so many of us after 9/11. How should we proceed? I found myself putting away my more ironic, caustic, full-of-clever writing. Of all of my projects, *Pieces of April* was the only one that seemed necessary.

Maybe it was also a product of getting older. Look at Almodóvar! Look at *Talk to Her* and then look at his early films. *Talk to Her* is a masterpiece. Even from *All About My Mother* to *Talk to Her* he makes a seismic leap. In *All About My Mother*, you feel him moving the people in a way that I really admire, but then *Talk to Her* comes along and it's as if the people in the movie are moving *him*. I'm thinking, "Whoa! My god! *This* is possible?" It made me want to keep working and working, in hopes that one day I might make something as accomplished.

It took a long time to find a story that I had to tell. I have boxes of abandoned screenplays. I kept reaching a point where I'd go, who needs this one? I'm already bored. So it's an interesting question. When does that moment come when one goes, I have to tell this story, as opposed to a million other stories?

Rob: Do you have perspective on what you do, do you think?

Peter: Not always. That's why other people are so important. And not always people who agree with or like what I do. When I wrote *Gilbert Grape*, many people challenged the ending. They said, You can't burn down a house with a 500-pound woman inside who had just passed away. I knew it was right, but other people's doubt drove me to earn the ending. This was also true with the end of *Pieces of April*, where many people said, "You can't stop the story here. We have to see the scene where they reunite and hear what they have to say to each other." But we knew that we didn't need that scene.

Rob: *That would have been gross.*

Peter: Well, it's a good sign that it's gross and all wrong when you try to write it and every word makes you cringe. Sanford Meisner, who was my acting teacher after I got out of college, said the most important thing anybody has ever said to me, in terms of the work. He said, "Peter, do you want to be a good actor?"

I said, "Well, a good actor would be fine, but I really want to be a writer."

He said, "Okay, do you want to be a *good* writer? Do you want to be a good person? Do you want to learn how to love? Do you want to be an artist of life?"

I said "Yes, to all of those things. That would be really swell."

He said, "Twenty years. Anything worth doing well will take you twenty years to learn. And in your case, Peter, maybe twenty-one."

It was a very freeing concept for me because I had been so ambitious as an actor and it had gone so poorly and, once I started writing, I wanted things to come too quickly. He said, "Look, you may become famous, you may become successful, you may become rich, but you can't be good at anything worth doing well for twenty years." I've been writing now nineteen and a half years, and I'm sticking to the "maybe twenty-one" concept. So, I have a year and a half to get some things figured out.

Sanford Meisner taught me that I didn't have to be in a hurry. But he was also clear that I'd have to work hard every day.

Rob: *That sense can come from having to pay your rent, too, though.*

Peter: Yes, and also if you have some morbid sense that you're not going to live long, which I've had all my life. I can't believe I'm still here. I don't know why. A lot of writers I admire have a heightened sense of their own mortality. Tennessee Williams, after he wrote *Glass Menagerie*, called his friends and said, "I'm not writing anymore, I'm dying, come say goodbye." Of course, not only did he live, the next thing he wrote was *A Streetcar Named Desire*. There's a relationship between that fear of mortality and the creative process, especially when you're really close to finishing something. It's at those times I feel so alive, I just know something could happen that will stop me from finishing this project. I always know I must be doing pretty good work when that occurs—or, at least, I've conned myself into believing it.

Rob: **About a Boy** *was an adaptation . . .*

Peter: Of the Nick Hornby novel. I was hired when there was no director. My first draft that was very true to the book, with one caveat—they asked me to make Will an American, which is probably why they hired me. We were always prepared to turn him back to an Englishman. When I do an adaptation—certainly this was true for *About a Boy* and *A Map of the World*—I tend to love the source material so much that, if it all came from the book and there was not a moment of my own creation in it, that would be more than fine with me. The proudest moment of my entire involvement with *About a Boy* was the phone call that Nick Hornby made to me after the first draft to say that he was pleased. When I heard that the Weitz brothers were going to direct, I thought, they're not going to need me, because they're terrific writers, and the truth was they didn't need me. They made great changes. They put in voice-over, cut the Kurt Cobain subplot, and invented a completely new third act. The credit for *About a Boy* mostly goes to Nick Hornby's story and the Weitz brothers' lovely film. I learned a lot from what they did. Mainly to not be so precious with source material. My version of *About a Boy* would probably have been darker. I still think it would have been funny, because if you adapt *About a Boy* and it's not funny, you have no talent. There's so much beauty and love in the way Nick Hornby writes, and I think the world is aching to laugh right now, and be ennobled with humor. I think that movie was very successful in that regard, and it's nice to have been a small part of it. Getting to live in Nick Hornby's prose for a year and a half was a pretty good job.

Rob: **Pieces of April** *was influenced by a very difficult life experience you had, which is particularly interesting because it was also the first original screenplay you would try to make, let alone direct.*

Peter: One approach to dealing with untenable life situations—and, certainly, my mother's death was as untenable as I've ever encountered—is to make something, to try and make meaning out of it. I didn't want to cannibalize my life or her experience. I didn't keep a journal during that time. But I did know that the one thing the dying teach the living—and, certainly what my mother taught me—is that it's coming for all of us, and what is it in your life that, if you don't do, you'll regret? Regret is such a driving force, and the gift of the cancer death is that you're given time. You don't know how much time, but you're given the chance to try and make memories, and ultimately the chance to say "Thank you, I'm sorry, and good-bye." All of this impacted the writing of *Pieces of April*. These people are running out of time and, if they weren't, they wouldn't be spending any time together. It is that inexorable tick-tock of life that is throwing them together.

I think anytime you make your first movie, it's full of all sorts of emotion—I can't imagine that it wouldn't be—but for me it's doubly so because this project has been made in response to my mother's death. The thing that surprised me was how much humor she had, how much rage there was, how little self-pity, and how the violins of Camille never played underneath. There was a lot of stainless steel, and a lot of plastic and pills, and it was a lot of florescent lights. It wasn't anything like how I've seen death portrayed in film. I wanted very much to make a story that reflected a more life-like experience. Another thing, there were so many occasions going on—Easter, tulips in her garden, her last birthday—where we were seeking ways to make beautiful moments because we knew there was going to come a time when we would no longer be able to. Some of it was selfish, like I want to have these good memories so I won't feel terrible. Some of it is also the hard truth that we all die alone. You can be surrounded with love, but, if you're dying, you're the only one who's dying. That was the other thing that became really clear—as much as we wanted to make it as beautiful and pleasant for her as possible, the fact was she didn't want to die. But she did.

Rob: I'm thinking about modern American life, and there's a sub-plot in Gilbert Grape *about Burger Barn infringing on the local, small town experience. In* About a Boy, *albeit an adaptation, there's the theme that no man is an island—he's got his espresso machine, stereo, etc., but it's not enough. I was thinking about the way people die in hospitals now, machinery, stainless steel, and plastic. My grandmother was recently in the hospital, and the sounds, electronics, and gadgets involved for her to simply sit up and eat something . . .*

I think there's a tension that exists in modern life between some type of organic experience, of being organically connected to each other, and all the modern trappings, which you hit on frequently.

Peter: This is a country of stuff. We just have so much stuff, and there is a war between how one lives authentically and all the trappings that surround us. And death is big business. Food is big business. Childhood, oh my God! It wasn't until I became a parent that I realized how the battle for their attention, for their souls, begins at practically their first breath. There's this incessant message on television, in the papers, in the air. If you just had *this*, then everything would be okay. So we're constantly being sold. They're selling us a war right now. I just think that's probably what draws me to the Burger Barn, or to stopping off at Krispy Kreme to get a doughnut, as they do in *April*. It's my way to navigate through what you can't avoid. We are consumers. It's either consume or be consumed. It's one of the fascinating parts of having made *Pieces of April*. I've explained some of what this story means to me, but now it's become a product. Smart people are spending long hours trying to figure out ways to convince you to choose this movie as opposed to some other movie. Obviously I want people to see it, so I'm invested in how it's marketed and how it will live in the world. But it's curious that while I'm raging against how everything is for sale, I'm also hoping people will buy a ticket to my movie.

Rob: You said before that people were giving you difficulty about how **Pieces of April** *ended, when I think the story arc would have been thrown off balance if you had gone further. The journey of the film is only to get you to that moment, and then you're done. Anything further would have ruined it.*

Peter: Yes, but they've come around. Look, this movie was set up and fell apart three different times. Lots of people doubted whether it should even be made. It took a fourth try—the ultra-low budget approach, sixteen-day shoot—to finally get it done. So the ending was only a small part of our troubles. And now we've made a movie with an ending that's earned. It's not false, there are no shortcuts. These characters fight to get a moment of grace, and they get it. Even that passes, though. We cut to black at the end and it's over, and of course she's going to die, and of course it was just a moment.

But it's so strange to feel like I have to apologize because it evokes a sincere and, at times, significant emotional response from people. At Sundance I actually started to worry that it might be a lesser movie if people really liked it. But the truth is, the world's on fire these days. It's out of control, and here's a movie that isn't adding to the madness.

Rob Feld began his life in New York film and theater working under legendary director Wynn Handman at the American Place Theater. Graduating Cornell University in 1996, studying Intellectual History, Feld worked at Vanguard Films, under producer John Williams, on such films as *Seven Years in Tibet* and *Shrek*.

Striking out on his own, Feld began freelancing in New York's indie film scene, eventually joining the New York and London based production company Manifesto Films as producer and Head of Production. Feld has written screenplays for production companies such as Vanguard, and his industry analysis, essays, and interviews appear frequently in the Writers Guild of America's monthly magazine, *Written By*.

Feld first met Peter Hedges at the Sundance Film Festival when *Pieces of April* premiered, and conducted a series of interviews with Hedges between February and July 2003, in Hedges' office in Brooklyn Heights, New York.

CAST AND CREW CREDITS

United Artists and IFC Productions present an InDigEnt production in association with Kalkaska Productions

PIECES OF APRIL

Written and Directed by
PETER HEDGES

Produced by
JOHN LYONS

Produced by
GARY WINICK
ALEXIS ALEXANIAN

Executive Producers
JONATHAN SEHRING
CAROLINE KAPLAN
JOHN SLOSS

Co-Producers
LUCY BARZUN
LUCILLE MASONE SMITH

Associate Producer
DIANNE DREYER

Director of Photography
TAMI REIKER

Production Designer
RICK BUTLER

Editor
MARK LIVOLSI

Costume Designer
LAURA BAUER

Music by
STEPHIN MERRITT

Executive Music Producer
ALEX STEYERMARK

Music Supervisor
LINDA COHEN

Casting
BERNARD TELSEY, CSA
DAVID VACCARI
WILL CANTLER, CSA

Katie Holmes   Patricia Clarkson   Derek Luke   Alison Pill

John Gallagher, Jr.   Alice Drummond   Lillias White   Isiah Whitlock, Jr.

SisQo   Armando Riesco   with Sean Hayes and Oliver Platt

Unit Production Manager . . . . Lucille Masone Smith	Parade Announcer . . . . Marcus Lovett
First Assistant Director . . . . Vebe Borge	Lee Quong . . . . Jack Chen
Second Assistant Director. . . . . Augie Carton	Lee Lang . . . . Jacqueline Dai
	Lee Wai Yam . . . . Rosa Luo
CAST IN ORDER OF APPEARANCE	Woman Outside Bodega . . . . Birdie M. Hale
April Burns . . . . Katie Holmes	Tyrone. Armando Riesco
Bobby. . . . . Derek Luke	Waitress . . . . Christine Todino
Jim Burns . . . . Oliver Platt	Young Mother . . . . Anney Giobbe
Beth Burns . . . . Alison Pill	Young Girl. . . . . Elizabeth Douglass
Timmy Burns . . . . John Gallagher, Jr.	Joy's Biker Guy . . . . Rusty DeWees
Joy Burns . . . . Patricia Clarkson	Timmy's Biker Guy. . . . . Vincent Roselli
Grandma Dottie . . . . Alice Drummond	
Half Asleep Man. . . . . Vitali Baganov	Post-Production Supervisor. . . . . Jake Abraham
Evette . . . . Lillias White	Art Directors . . . . Shannon Robert Bowen
Eugene . . . . Isiah Whitlock, Jr.	Aleta Shaffer
Man in Mohair Sweater . . . . Adrian Martinez	Script Supervisor. . . . . Dianne Dreyer
Tish. . . . . Susan Bruce	B Camera Operator. . . . . Sam Levy
Boy on Bicycle. . . . . Jamari Richardson	First Assistant Camera . . . . Nathaniel Miller
Woman in Stairwell . . . . Leila Danette	Second Assistant Camera . . . . Jason Vandermer
Lee Loung Tan . . . . Stephen Chen	Assistant Costume Designer . . . . Bobby Tilley
Lee Quong Tan. . . . . Sally Leung Bayer	Wardrobe Supervisor . . . . Amy Burt
Wayne . . . . Sean Hayes	Hair Department Heads. . . . . Julie Delaney
Latrell . . . . SisQo	HolliPops Smith

Make-Up Department Head . . . . Mike Potter
Gaffer . . . . Kate Phelan
                       Graham Willoughby
Key Grip . . . . Cat Crosby
Sound Mixer . . . . Aaron Rudelson
Boom Operator . . . . Bryant Musgrove
Location Manager . . . . Jeff Brown
Production Coordinator . . . . Kerin Ferallo
Production Accountant . . . . Matilde Valera
Post Production Accountant . . . . Mara Connolly
Casting Associates . . . . Jaclyn Brodsky
                       Craig Burns
Still Photographer . . . . Teddy Maki
Assistant Production Coordinator . . . . . Beth M. Schniebolk
Assistant Art Director . . . . Steph Brynner
On-Set Dresser . . . . Shane Klein
Set Dresser . . . . Betsy Baker
Scenic Artists . . . . Christina Polumbo
                       Tim C. Okamura
                       Devin Butler
Graphic Artist . . . . Leo Holder
Set Production Assistants . . . . Paul Polow
                       Adrian Correia
               Thomas "Bravo" Roughan
Assistant Locations Manager . . . . Matthew Longwell
Locations Scout . . . . Tom Polleri
Locations Assistants . . . . Dave Hall
                       Josh Newport
Locations Consultant . . . . Jonathan Roumie
Key Make-Up . . . . Joanna J. Stewart
Art Department Assistant . . . . Jim Simak
Office Production Assistant . . . . R. Berndt Mader
Assistant to John Lyons . . . . Peter Friedlander
Production Coordinator . . . . Mandy Tagger
Interns . . . . Bettina Bilger
             Chika I. Chukudebelu
                       Emily Hart
                  Sebastian Ischer
              Richard S. Kaplinski
                       Marion Koh
                       Karrie Myers
                       Taylor Roe
                       Brian Sachson
                       Adele Thaxton
Catering . . . . Shooting Stars Catering
                   Brian & Lisa Brown
                       Kevin McGill
Assistant Editor . . . . Rachel Biles
Post-Production Coordinator . . . . Emily Gardiner
Production Legal . . . . Sloss Law Office L.L.P.
               Jacqueline Eckhouse, Esq.
                 Jennifer Gaylord, Esq.

Post Production Sound Services by . . . . 701 Sound
                   Marlena Grzaslewicz
                       Ira Spiegel
                     Mariusz Glabinski
                       Piotr Glabinski
Music Editor . . . . Alison LaCourse
Post-Production Sound Mixing and ADR . . . .
                Sound One Corporation
Re-Recording Mixer . . . . Robert Fernandez
Dolby Sound Consultant . . . . Steve F.B. Smith
AVID services provided by . . . . Orbit Digital
Titles by . . . . 280 Design
Color Correction by . . . . Moving Images
Colorists . . . . Milan Boncich
                       Carlos Rodriguez
Tape to Film . . . . Swiss Effects
Supervising . . . . Ruedi Schick
Shooting . . . . David Pfluger
Production Insurance by . . . . AON/Albert G. Ruben
Payroll Services by . . . . Entertainment Partners
Public Relations by . . . . Magic Lantern Inc.
Financing and Distribution Advisory Services . . Cinetic Media
Filmed on location in: . . . . New York City
                 Bear Mountain, New York
                    Blauvelt, New York
                      Sparkill, New York
                 East Meadow, New York
                West Caldwell, New Jersey

Properties and Furniture Courtesy of
Jack Marcus Brodsky & Family

Paintings in April's apartment by Tim C. Okamura

Sculpture in April's apartment by Denise Carbonnelle

Ceramic Turkeys courtesy of Carole Hedges

"Bernadette the Dog" played by Ficchi,
courtesy of Maria Maggenti

Production Resources . . . . Wendy Cohen

Wigs by Mike Potter

Make-Up Provided by M·A·C

Chinese Dance Television Footage courtesy of
Oddball Film and Video

"I Think I Need A New Heart"
Written by Stephin Merritt
Performed by The Magnetic Fields
Courtesy of Merge Records

"The Well Tempered Guitar"
Written by J.S. Bach
Performed by John Woo

145

"Aphrodisiac"
Written by Dave Mann and Emmanuel Kallins
Performed by Studio Musicians
Courtesy of FirstCom Music, Inc.

"You You You You You"
Written by Stephin Merritt
Performed by The 6ths
Courtesy of Merge Records

"Baby Won't You Tell Me"
Written by Steve Fawcett
Performed by Studio Musicians
Courtesy of FirstCom Music, Inc.

"Liberty Bell March"
Written by Randall Crissman and Michael Babcock
Performed by Studio Musicians
Courtesy of FirstCom Music, Inc.

"The Luckiest Guy On The Lower East Side"
Written by Stephin Merritt
Performed by The Magnetic Fields
Courtesy of Merge Records

"Salsa Brava"
Written by Charlie D'Cali
Performed by Charlie D'Cali Orquesta
Courtesy of Charlie D'Cali

"Xiqing"
Traditional, arrangement by Cheng Yu
Performed by The UK Chinese Ensemble
Courtesy of FirstCom Music, Inc.

"Hymn Of Peace"
Written by E. Dozor
Performed by Studio Musicians
Courtesy of Killer Tracks

"Epitaph For My Heart"
Written by Stephin Merritt
Performed by The Magnetic Fields
Courtesy of Merge Records

"Jolly Old St. Nick"
Traditional, arrangement by Alex Constantine
Performed by Alex Constantine
Courtesy of Killer Tracks

"Deck The Halls"
Traditional, arrangement by Johnny Sedona
Performed by Johnny Sedona
Courtesy of Killer Tracks

"As You Turn To Go"
Written by Stephin Merritt
Performed by The 6ths
Courtesy of Merge Records

THANKS TO:
Action Camera Cars: Stephen Mann
Amana
Arthur's Dress Shop, Berrain Eno-Van Fleet
Aperture Magazine
Barbizon Lighting Company, Adrienne Patsos
Blauvelt Coach Diner, Peter Krimitsos & Staff
Bumble & bumble
Butterball Turkeys
Camera Service Center, Hardwrick Johnson & Charlie Tammaro
Coca-Cola Company
COLOR WHEEL
Entertainment Partners, Eric Shonz & Myfa Cirinna
Greenbush Presbyterian Church, Bruce Page
Kiehl's
Kings Korner Gifts Scottsburg, Indiana, Belinda Houchens
Kodak
Krispy Kreme of East Meadow, New York, Brian Fiarello
Meow Mix NYC, Brooke Webster & Andrew Cathcart
Metro Concepts Music
Movie Time Cars
Notre Dame Church
NYC Parks, Elaine Crowley
New Jersey Film Commission
New York City Mayor's Office For Film, Theatre & Broadcasting, Patricia Reed Scott, Commissioner; Jane P. Brawley, Deputy Commissioner
Randy's Garage, Randy Johnson
Screen Actors Guilld
Ocean Spray Company
Organic and Natural Food Market, Tomas Crespo
The Palisades Interstate Park Commission, Bear Mountain, New York: Stephanie Broadnax
Patmont Motor Works, Tim Patmont
The Puck Building, Larry Schwartz & Jaime Marks
The Salvation Army, Frankie Hailey & Major Lawrence Shaffer
St. Thomas Aquinas College, Vin Crapanzano
Suffolk Realty Corp.
Town of Orangetown, New York
Township of West Caldwell, New Jersey
Willis Avenue United Methodist Church, Rev. Harold W. Morris, Sr.
Xeno Lights, Scott Ramsey & Chris Barra

SPECIAL THANKS TO:
Dr. Steve Abraham
Gary Baker
Susan Batten
Kamau Benjamin
Dr. Carl Berg
Merri Biechler
Stephen Breimer
Joannie Burstein
Diana Burton

Niamh Butler
Joseph Calritos
The Cata Family
Justin Christopher
Ana Cintron
Joe Dapello
Chris Delosangeles
Steve Dontanville
Mary Clare Evans
Anthony Famigietti
Marc H. Glick
Wendy Goidell
Claudia Gonson
Kenny Goodman
Richard Greenberg
Desmond Guthrie
Lucas Hedges
Rev. Robert B. and Laurel Hedges
Simon Hedges
Karl Heiselman
Brandt Joel
Susan King
Scott Laule
Michael Leslie
Rich & Jill Lichtig
Ken Lipper
Austin Lopez
Derrick Loris
Tod A. Maitland
Ryan McMahon
Lisa, Megan and Douglas McWilliams
Tory Metzger
Ruth Moore
Mary-Louise Parker
Michael Peretzian
Bob Ricca
Ann Roth

Carin Sage
Kirsten Schatz
Ira Schreck
Eric Scott
Mike Scott
Raymond T. Shelton
David Shuchat
Sydney Sidner
Alin Splichel
Erwin Stoff
John & Narcissa Titman
Lesley Topping
Sally Willcox
Jim Zachar
Elan, Scott, Ira, and all the tenants of 176 Suffolk Street

Pieces of April

A Peter Hedges Film

in memory of
my mother,
Carole Hedges,
who loved every day

ABOUT THE FILMMAKER

PETER HEDGES adapted his first novel, *What's Eating Gilbert Grape*, for director Lasse Hallström. His second novel was *An Ocean in Iowa*. His other screenplay adaptations include *A Map of the World* and *About a Boy*, which was nominated for an Academy Award® for Best Adapted Screenplay. Also a playwright, Hedges' plays include *Baby Anger*, *Good as New*, and *Imagining Brad*. *Pieces of April* marks his directorial debut. He lives in Brooklyn, New York, with his wife and two children.